Praise for Debra Gordon Zaslow

"Some tellers only tell a story, but Debra enlightens the story, infusing it with extra light, wisdom and power." —**Jane Yolen**, author, *Favorite Folktales from Around the World*

"Debra Zaslow is a modern maggidah…the way she moves from the tale to her reflection is a wonderful example of how we can best internalize the seemingly simple tales to heal our complicated lives." —**Rabbi Zalman Schachter-Shalomi** *z"l*, founder of ALEPH: Alliance for Jewish Renewal

"Debra has a way of looking life in the eye—a courage and sense of humor that invite us directly into her world." —**Jay O'Callahan**, storyteller, author, *The Spirit of the Great Auk*

Praise for *The Rooster Princess and Other Tales*

"The stories we tell are a reflection of who we are and who we dream of becoming. These stories are rich and resonant with women's voices and values, at once familiar and entirely new. Like all great folk tales, Chelm stories, and fables, they teach us and inspire us to feel. I look forward to returning to these tales again and again, and sharing them with generations to come." —**Rachel Barenblat**, "The Velveteen Rabbi," and author of *Texts to the Holy*

"A collection of fascinating and profound folktales embedded with the wisdom of Jewish values. The strong women characters have replaced males with appropriateness and integrity. This brings a new perspective to mirror our lives and deepens the meaning of our folklore." —**Peninnah Schram**, author of *Jewish Stories One Generation Tells Another* and *Stories within Stories: From the Jewish Oral Tradition*

"*The Rooster Princess and Other Tales* is a much needed and highly recommended collection of stories that puts women front and center in Jewish folklore. The stories range from the biblical Eve to Edel, the daughter of the Baal Shem Tov, to Hannah of Chelm, as well as including contemporary personal stories. What an excellent resource for teachers, storytellers, and readers who will delight and be inspired by these stories that place women in leading roles while staying true to the meaning of the original tales." —**Barbara Diamond Goldin**, coauthor of *Meet Me at the Well*: *The Girls and Wise Women of the Bible*, with Jane Yolen

"*The Rooster Princess and Other Tales* is filled with heroines from countless times and places who are strong, capable and brave. Taken altogether, they form the book's kaleidoscopic view of Jewish females and the feminine. Both women and men need to read *The Rooster Princess* to learn the women's wisdom that shines through the tales and into our hearts." —**Cherie Karo Schwartz**, author of *Circle Spinning*: *Jewish Turning and Returning Tales*

"The fresh feminine perspective found in *The Rooster Princess* will both tickle and uplift its readers. This is a much needed treasury of women's tales, containing voices that have gone missing from Jewish literature for far too long." —**Rabbi Tirzah Firestone, PhD**, author of *The Receiving*: *Reclaiming Jewish Women's Wisdom*

The Rooster Princess
And Other Tales

Jewish Stories Re-populated with Spunky Heroines, Wise Women, Brave Crones, and Powerful Prophetesses

Jewish Women's Storytelling Collective

Edited by Debra Gordon Zaslow
with Gail Pasternack and Deborah Rosenberg

MONKFISH
BOOK PUBLISHING COMPANY
RHINEBECK, NEW YORK

The Rooster Princess and Other Tales: Jewish Stories Re-populated with Spunky Heroines, Wise Women, Brave Crones, and Powerful Prophetesses Copyright © 2025 by Debra Gordon Zaslow

All rights reserved. No part of this book may be used or reproduced in any manner, excerpt in critical articles or reviews. Contact the publisher for information.

Paperback ISBN 9781958972878
eBook ISBN 9781958972885

Library of Congress Cataloging-in-Publication Data

Names: Jewish Women's Storytelling Collective (Ashland, Oregon), author. | Zaslow, Debra Gordon, editor. | Pasternack, Gail, editor. | Rosenberg, Deborah, editor.
Title: The rooster princess and other tales : Jewish stories re-populated with spunky heroines, wise women, brave crones, and powerful prophetesses / Jewish Women's Storytelling Collective ; edited by Debra Gordon Zaslow ; with Gail Pasternack and Deborah Rosenberg.
Description: Rhinebeck, New York : Monkfish Book Publishing Company, 2025.
Identifiers: LCCN 2025017579 (print) | LCCN 2025017580 (ebook) | ISBN 9781958972878 (paperback) | ISBN 9781958972885 (ebook)
Subjects: LCSH: Women in Judaism. | Tales--Adaptations. | Jewish women in literature.
Classification: LCC BM729.W6 J495 2025 (print) | LCC BM729.W6 (ebook) | DDC 296.082--dc23/eng/20250418
LC record available at https://lccn.loc.gov/2025017579
LC ebook record available at https://lccn.loc.gov/2025017580

Book and cover design by Colin Rolfe
Cover art by Cassandra זהרה Sagan

Monkfish Book Publishing Company
22 East Market Street, Suite 304
Rhinebeck, New York 12572
(845) 876-4861
monkfishpublishing.com

This book is dedicated to Peninnah Schram, and Roslyn Bresnick-Perry *z"l*, the storytelling mavens who graciously welcomed me into the world of Jewish storytelling and inspired me to create my own niche. —DGZ

The Jewish Women's Storytelling Collective began in 2022 when Debra Gordon Zaslow and five female graduates of her *maggid* (Jewish storyteller and Torah teacher) training program expressed frustration with the lack of female protagonists in Jewish folklore. They decided to create a new story collection by replacing male characters with females. This anthology evolved into including original tales, Torah narratives, and personal stories. Over the next two years, five more *maggidot* (plural for female *maggidah*) joined by adding their adapted and original stories. The shared vision of the Jewish Women's Storytelling Collective is to offer Jewish stories from a uniquely female perspective and to make those stories accessible to modern audiences.

Debra Gordon Zaslow
Gail Pasternack
Deborah Rosenberg
Lisa Huberman
José de Kwaadsteniet
Cyrise Beatty Schachter
Cassandra Sagan
Batya Podos
Ayala Sarah Zonnenschein
Melissa Carpenter
Rivkah Coburn

Contents

Introduction | *Debra Gordon Zaslow*   xi

PART ONE
Wise Women

Sarika and the Magic Pomegranate Seed | *Gail Pasternack*   3
The Trouble with the Spoon | *Deborah Rosenberg*   9
Edel's Spark | *Lisa Huberman*   13
A Woman and a Sultan | *José de Kwaadsteniet*   17
Secret of the Chanukah Flame | *Debra Gordon Zaslow*   20
Hannah and the Moon | *Gail Pasternack*   26
The Thirty-Sixth Night of Chanukah | *Cassandra Sagan*   30

PART TWO
Mothers and Daughters

The Mountain and the Cliff | *Rivkah Coburn*   37
The Little Magpie | *Lisa Huberman*   40
Journey of the Lost Princess | *Debra Gordon Zaslow*   46
My Mother's Candlesticks | *José de Kwaadsteniet*   51
A Forgiveness Story | *Debra Gordon Zaslow*   55

PART THREE
Freedom to Be Oneself

The Rooster Princess | *Lisa Huberman*   63
The Day Elijah Saved My Life | *Batya Podos*   68
Holding Her Own | *Debra Gordon Zaslow*   73

The Fishmonger and the Shiviti | *Ayala Sarah Zonnenschein*   76
The Shekhinah Is in Exile | *Debra Gordon Zaslow*   81
A Queer Soul in the Shtetl | *Lisa Huberman*   84

PART FOUR
Gifts We Give and Receive

Esperanza and the Twelve Loaves of Challah | *Gail Pasternack*   95
Bella's Beautiful Coat | *Deborah Rosenberg*   100
Chana Seeks a Treasure | *Debra Gordon Zaslow*   106
Flour in the Wind | *Gail Pasternack*   110
From Feather to Feather | *Cassandra Sagan*   114
Emptying Cups | *Gail Pasternack*   119

PART FIVE
Torah Women

They Will Call Me Naamah | *Batya Podos*   125
Serach bat-Asher, the Story | *José de Kwaadsteniet*   130
Miriam Chats with God | *Melissa Carpenter*   134
Tears Before the Gate | *José de Kwaadsteniet*   139

PART SIX
Supernatural Stories

House of the Demons' Weddings | *Deborah Rosenberg*   145
Rachel and the Enchanted Spring | *Gail Pasternack*   150
A Charm in the Red Dress | *Deborah Rosenberg*   155
The Day the Shtetl Wept | *Cyrise Beatty Schachter*   161
Angel in the Candle Flame | *Cassandra Sagan*   169
An Honored Guest | *Deborah Rosenberg*   173

Contributors   177
Acknowledgements   181

Introduction

DEBRA GORDON ZASLOW

A FEW years ago, to stave off boredom at the beginning of the pandemic, I started working on storytelling with my twelve-year-old granddaughter. After she chose a Jewish story to learn, we began to visualize the characters in her story. When asked to describe how she saw Elijah the prophet, she said, without hesitation, "I see a woman."

I was floored. As a storyteller whose specialty is stories with strong female characters, I'm well aware there is a lack of powerful female imagery in all of folk literature. I also know it's crucial to visualize characters fully to transmit clear images to the audience, so listeners can identify with story characters. But my granddaughter's response illustrated the cognitive dissonance so viscerally that I was stunned.

After over a decade of secular storytelling, when I ventured into Jewish stories in the mid-1980s, I was surprised at how difficult it was to find Jewish tales featuring powerful female characters. This seemed ironic, given the obvious strength of Jewish women. Over the years, I found myself slipping some female characters into the stories and changing a few male protagonists into females. Why not? My criterion was simple: if it didn't change the basic meaning or plot of the story, the character could be female. There was always the sense, however, of meddling with something sacrosanct. These

Jewish stories have been handed down for centuries, and who was I to change them?

At the same time, I was familiar with the deep effect that oral storytelling has on listeners. I often describe storytelling as a "contact sport." When a teller puts forth imagery, she senses the audience receiving it in a kind of "story trance" as the feelings go back and forth between the teller and the listeners. Our body of folk literature, carrying the key values of our culture, is thus absorbed deeply in a new dance with each audience.

Furthermore, the depth of that absorption depends on how much the listeners identify with the story characters. Carl Jung, Bruno Bettelheim, and other psychologists have written extensively about the power of identification with archetypal characters. Briefly, if we see ourselves in the heroes as they slay huge dragons or resolve little problems, we draw a vicarious satisfaction that helps us deal with our own inner conflicts. If the hero is always male, though, half of the audience will have trouble joining in the symbolic struggles and victories. I wanted to give my listeners a storytelling experience that was not only enlightening, but also one they could personally relate to.

When I started training *maggid* (Jewish storyteller and Torah teacher) students in 2009 with my husband, Rabbi David Zaslow, the majority of our students were female. My first instruction to students is always to find a story that resonates with them. As my students perused the stories, it was painfully evident, yet again, that women were mostly absent from the core tales that impart the values of our culture and religion.

Of course, over the years there has been a shift in the interpretation of Jewish scripture, and in spiritual leadership. Women are being ordained as Rabbis in increasing numbers, and for several years women have been publishing works with female interpretations of the Torah. New creative imaginings (*midrash*) of biblical women have emerged from our rabbis and poets. In 2016, Yael Kanarek conceived *Torah Ta* (Her Torah), with a Torah written with all the gender roles reversed. This parallels a paradigm shift across cultures and religions that allows women, for the first time, to see themselves reflected in an image of the divine.

However, despite all the feminization of Torah interpretation, with even the Torah itself rewritten in a reverse-gender form, there are still no new forms of classic Jewish folklore. In every culture the stories of the people provide food for ingesting values and traditions. Yet, all the Jewish stories written by and about men have been passed down for centuries with little change. While there are a couple of anthologies of Jewish stories that feature women, they are very few in comparison with the large body of Jewish stories.

In 2019, after reading a collection of stories of the Baal Shem Tov (the eighteenth-century rabbi who founded Hasidism), our maggid-student cohort expressed their dismay at the lack of female protagonists and the apparent sexism of many of the stories. It seemed like it was time to do something, and the germ of an idea for this collection was born.

Although I'd been slipping female characters into oral stories for years, as I'm sure other storytellers have done, I was hesitant to commit that experiment to print. The haunting question of *Who am I to change the sacred tradition?* remained. However, when I witnessed my granddaughter's innocent effort to imagine a major Jewish character as female, it became obvious that these changes needed to be published, and an answer emerged. *Who am I?* A Jewish storyteller, that's who. And my colleagues and I have the responsibility and privilege to provide a turning point for future generations of storytellers, readers, and listeners.

Each woman in our Jewish Women's Storytelling Collective has graduated from our training program as a *maggidah* (female storyteller). Collectively they are *maggidot*. They have contributed a variety of regendered stories to this collection, along with some original stories and personal stories. Our diversity includes a range of ages, gender identities, and sexual orientation. We live on the West Coast, East Coast, Southwest, and one even in the Netherlands. We are not only storytellers, but also poets, visual artists, theatre professors, dancers, Torah teachers, rabbinic students, musicians, day-school teachers, and most importantly, each of us is an innovative, risk-taking feminist.

Our goal is to offer a fresh collection that includes traditional stories teaching basic Jewish and universal human values while featuring female characters in the central roles. The purpose of this anthology is not to eliminate the stories that highlight male characters, but to offer an alternative version that is equally inspiring to girls and women. It was important that we did not change the basic meaning of the traditional stories and that we acknowledge their sources. We hope female readers will see themselves reflected in the variety of roles in these stories, and that all readers will savor the restoration of balance to Jewish folk literature.

I recently told a re-gendered Chanukah story ("Secret of the Chanukah Flame") at a gathering at a local senior center. After the telling, a sixty-year-old woman stood with her arm around her ninety-year-old mother. "I've heard that story before," she told me, "But it feels different now." Both of them had tears streaming down their faces. Our hope is that tears flow down the faces of women everywhere as they begin to see themselves in the compelling stories of our people.

PART ONE
Wise Women

Sarika and the Magic Pomegranate Seed

GAIL PASTERNACK

THERE WAS once a girl named Sarika who lived in the Jewish quarter of Fez in Morocco with her parents and three younger sisters. Her father was a gifted metal craftsman who drew clients from all over Fez for his elaborate serving platters and dishware. In another city, he would have earned a nice living, but, sadly, most of his profits went to pay the high taxes imposed on them by the sultan.

To earn more money and help feed the family, Sarika and her mother cleaned the home of a wealthy family in town. Sarika never loved cleaning. She always rushed through her work and scurried home to help her father in his shop. No matter how busy he was, he took the time to teach Sarika the skills of his trade. She enjoyed the music their chisel and hammer made as they worked together, and she glowed from his compliments when she finished each piece.

One morning, Sarika and her mother passed through the gates of the Jewish quarter walls. They wound their way through the narrow streets of Fez until they reached the peach stucco home of the wealthy family. They knocked on the heavy, wooden door as they always did, but no one opened it. They knocked again. Still no answer. Sarika's mother knocked a third time.

This time the woman of the house opened the door. She stood in the entrance, blocking Sarika and her mother from entering. "I'm sorry. I can no longer employ you. My husband was arrested for the crime of questioning the sultan in public." She stepped back and closed the door.

Sarika tugged at her mother's arm. "What about the wages she owes us for the past week? It's market day. We need that money."

Sarika's mother took a deep breath and stood tall. "We'll just have to barter."

Sarika and her mother headed to the city square where vendors had set up their colorful stalls. They were met by the scent of incense and the din of artisans hawking their wares.

Her mother approached the fish vendor. "What beautiful mackerel!" She smiled as the man puffed up with pride. "My daughter and I are expert seamstresses. We could do all your mending this week in exchange for just one fish."

The vendor's face darkened, and he took the fish from her hands. "Move along."

Her mother moved on to the baker's stall, and she offered to clean his house for a loaf of bread.

"No," the baker said.

When Sarika's mother spoke to a fruit vendor, who clearly had no interest in giving them anything, Sarika thought of her younger sisters and how they complained of not having enough to eat. She needed to do something.

As her mother kept the vendor engaged, Sarika took a pomegranate and slipped it into her pocket. Then she snuck over to a baker's stall and waited for the baker to engage in conversation with a customer. She grasped a loaf of bread, and just as she tucked it into her coat, someone grabbed her shoulder.

"Stop, thief!" a gruff voice said.

Sarika looked up into the face of a tall man wearing the uniform of the sultan's guard. He grabbed her with both hands and forced her out of the market.

Sarika's mother ran after them. "Please, please. Let her go! She's just a child."

The guard ignored her and took Sarika straight to a prison cell where the only light came from a small, iron-grated window. She was left in this dark, dank room for days. She had no visitors or any news of her fate. Nor did they bring her food. She dug her fingernails into the pomegranate and broke it open. Every day, she would eat a few seeds, careful to limit how much she ate so it could last.

One morning, the cell door opened, and a guard stood on the other side. "Time for your execution. The sultan has decided that your death will teach others not to steal."

The sun burned her eyes as Sarika was led out to the courtyard. The executioner unsheathed his curved sword.

Sarika slipped her shaking hand into her pocket where she kept her pomegranate. At that moment, she had an idea.

"Stealing is wrong, I know," she said. "I have earned my fate. But please do not waste this magic seed that's in my hand." She withdrew her hand from her pocket and opened it. In her palm was a single pomegranate seed.

The vizier stood from his seat next to the sultan. "Magic? Do you think we are fools? There is no such thing."

Sarika closed her hand. "If you're not interested …"

The vizier strode over to her. "What power does it possess?"

"If you plant it, it will immediately grow into a pomegranate tree, but no normal one. Anyone who eats its fruit will live a long life full of good fortune." She opened her hand again. "You sure you do not want it?"

The vizier reached for the seed, but before he could take it, Sarika closed her hand and withdrew it from him. "Be careful who you choose to plant it because the seed will only grow if it is planted by someone who has never stolen anything."

The vizier hung his head. "Then I cannot plant the seed. Once, on a cold night, I took a coat from my neighbor and never gave it back."

Sarika held her hand out to the head of the guard. "Perhaps you can plant this seed."

"I cannot," he said. "Once I was in such a hurry to deliver a message to the sultan that I took a man's horse. I should have gone back to the man's farm to return it, but I never did."

Sarika turned to the sultan. "Surely our exalted leader is the honest man who can plant this seed."

The sultan hung his head. "Sadly, no. This tree will not grow for me. I fought my brother after our father died. I took his life on the battlefield and usurped the title he had inherited."

"I never took a life or stole a title, a horse, or even a coat. I took a loaf of bread to feed my family. How is my crime worse?"

"It is not," the sultan said. "Tell me, why is such a clever girl so poor?"

Sarika knew her answer would seal her fate, and she would surely die at the hand of the executioner for expressing the cruelty of the sultan in front of his entourage. Still, it needed to be said. She stood her full height. "Your taxes, your highness. My father is a gifted artisan who makes the finest metalwork in all of Fez, but all he earns is sent to you."

The sultan's expression darkened. "Bring her father to me at once."

Sarika trembled. She couldn't bring her father to the sultan to be punished for her words, but she had no choice. Two guards seized her and took her to her father's shop. One strode through to the back, where Sarika's father was hammering fine details into a serving platter. Without any explanation, he grabbed her father's arm and marched him out onto the street, but the second guard lingered in the shop. He strolled through the aisles of serving platters and dishware on display, touching each piece as he passed. Then he took one plate and shoved it into his coat.

When they returned to the palace, the guards brought Sarika and her father to the throne room.

"Is his metalwork truly the finest in all of Fez?" the sultan asked the guards.

The second guard removed the dish from his coat and brought it to the sultan.

As the sultan inspected the dish, his expression remained impassive. "I cannot allow you to continue working as you do."

Sarika's father began to weep. His body shook with each sob.

Sarika lurched forward to join her father, but the first guard held her back. She struggled against the guard's grasp. "Please don't punish him for my wrongdoing. Punish me!"

The sultan held the dish up in the light streaming through the palace windows. He turned the plate one direction. Then the other. "How extraordinary." He passed his finger along the carvings, following the swoop of each curve. "I've never seen anything quite like it." He handed the dish back to the guard. "Is all of his work this exquisite?"

The guard nodded. "But this was the finest piece I saw in his workshop."

Sarika's father took a tentative step toward the guard. "May I see it?" The guard handed the dish to him, and Sarika's father held it up to the sun, letting the light shimmer on its surface. "I didn't make this." His eyes were still wet with tears, but he smiled at his daughter. "Sarika did."

The sultan and the guards all stared at Sarika. Their expressions were hard to read, but Sarika assumed that they were disgusted. They had to be. Everyone in Fez considered metalcraft a man's trade, not something for a girl to do.

"Don't blame my father for breaking custom." Sarika stood tall. "I take responsibility for all I have done wrong."

"No one this brave and talented should ever suffer from hunger," the sultan said. "Nor should anyone in her family."

He pardoned Sarika and hired her to be his personal metalworker. From that day forward, Sarika and her family never faced poverty again. And Sarika reveled in her life as a respected artisan.

ABOUT THE STORY

"Sarika and the Magic Pomegranate Seed" is based on a tale told by many storytellers. It is called "The Clever Thief" in José Patterson's book, *Angels, Prophets, Rabbis and Kings from the Stories of the Jewish People,* and "The Wise Thief" in Josepha Sherman's *A Sampler of Jewish American Folklore*. A version called "The Magic Seed" appears in Nina Jaffe and Steve Zeitlin's *The Cow of No Color: Riddle Stories and Justice Tales from Around the World,* and Sheldon Oberman's *Solomon and the Ant: And Other Jewish Folktales*. Peninnah Schram retells it as "The Pomegranate Seed" in her book, *The Hungry Clothes and Other Jewish Folktales*. In all versions, the thief is a man. I adapted the story to have a female protagonist and expanded it to capture the setting while filling in Sarika's backstory.

The Trouble with the Spoon

DEBORAH ROSENBERG

LIBKE RAN all the way home from school. When she left home that morning, her Mama had just begun to make the *cholent* for that night's Shabbat dinner. Libke loved cholent anyway, but on this remarkable Shabbat, her Mama had traded some of their eggs for a bit of lamb to celebrate the end of a long winter. Lamb! In the cholent!

When Libke rushed in, the tiny house smelled of everything that was good. Libke smelled the delicious combinations of three kinds of beans, onions, carrots, lots of paprika, and that succulent bit of lamb. She couldn't wait for candle lighting and for dinner.

Libke was in the small yard, feeding the chickens when she heard a scream from the kitchen. When she pulled open the back door, she saw a sight. Her Mama and her Auntie Bea stood on opposite sides of the kitchen, both staring at a wooden spoon lying in the ground.

Mama's eyes were wide open, and her mouth formed a wide O.

Auntie Bea wrung her hands over and over while she muttered, "Oh, no! Oh no! Oh, no!"

"What happened?!" Libke squeaked.

Mama and Auntie Bea began to talk at once. They sounded like the chickens! It took a few minutes before Libke could make sense of what they said.

"The spoon? The trouble is the spoon?"

Her aunt agreed. "I was stirring the rice and milk for tomorrow. I put the spoon on the plate, like always. Your mama—"

"I wasn't thinking. I wanted to stir the cholent, so I picked up the nearest spoon!" Mama wailed.

This was serious. A spoon that had been in milk could not be used to stir something that included a bit of meat. The cholent!

Libke whispered, "What will we do?"

Auntie Bea said, "We must ask the rabbi what to do. He will know. Libke, run!"

Libke ran. She ran through the village as fast as she could.

"Libke! What's the hurry?" her neighbor called.

"Can't stop, Mr. Goldstein. Need the rabbi!"

"Libke? What's the matter?"

"No time, Mrs. Rabinowitz! Cholent!"

"Libke? Where are you going?"

"Rabbi, Sarah. Emergency!"

When Libke finally got to the rabbi's house, she gasped and slapped her hand on the door. "Please, Mrs. Gottlieb, is the rabbi at home?"

The *rebbetzin* looked horrified. "Child! You're all red and—"

"I know, I ran, but please. It's an emergency!"

"I'll get you some water. Sit. I'll call the rabbi, but it's getting late. It's almost Shabbat. Don't keep him from his dinner."

Dinner? The cholent was in danger. Time was wasting. Libke tried to catch her breath.

Libke could breathe again by the time the rabbi came out with a book in his hands. "Yes, Libke? What's the trouble?" he asked kindly.

Libke stammered out the problem and waited, fidgeting, for the rabbi's decision.

"Interesting problem," said the rabbi. "We will find the answer. I have some questions. What direction was your mama standing when she stirred the cholent? East or west?"

"Rabbi, I don't know!"

"Well, well. Was your Auntie Bea wearing a blue apron or a white one?"

"Um, a blue one, maybe."

"Was the back door open or closed when the trouble began?"

"Closed, I think. I had to ... Rabbi? What do these questions matter?"

"Libke, you are a young girl, and I am the rabbi. That's why these questions matter." His eyebrows came together rather alarmingly. "In fact, this is a matter for your Mama and your Auntie Bea. Have them come see me tomorrow, after Shabbat. We will decide then."

The rabbi turned and left the room. Libke stood still, considering all she had heard. She left the house, carefully closing the door behind her, and then she ran.

She arrived again at home fearful of what she might find. It was possible that Mama or Auntie Bea might have given up waiting and destroyed the beautiful cholent. There was so much at stake! Libke again pulled open the back door. (Closed, she noted.) The house still smelled of simmering cholent, and Mama and Auntie Bea still stood helplessly in the kitchen.

"Well! What did the rabbi say?" demanded her Mama.

"So! What did the rabbi tell you?" demanded Auntie Bea.

Libke looked at her Mama. She looked at Auntie Bea. She looked at the troublesome spoon, still lying sadly where it had fallen. Libke took a big breath, of home, of Shabbat, and of that lovely spring cholent with a bit of lamb, and she decided for herself.

"We must burn the spoon, light the candles, and eat the cholent!"

And so, they did. It was delicious.

ABOUT THE STORY

I found this sweet story in the book, *Because God Loves Stories: An Anthology of Jewish Storytelling*, edited by Steve

Zeitlin. This was a story submitted by Matilda Friedman about her grandfather Isaac and how he learned to think for himself. In the spirit of our cause, I changed Grandfather Isaac to a girl named Libke and expanded the story to more fully tell this tale. I present it here with permission from Steve Zeitlin.

Edel's Spark

LISA HUBERMAN

EDEL ALWAYS knew she was special.

Her father, the great Baal Shem Tov, the founder of the Hasidic movement, used to tell her about how he picked her soul out from the book of Deuteronomy in the Torah. Just like God's presence shone like a "fiery law" onto the Israelites, so Edel's spirit blazed like a bright flame for all that encountered her.

While the daughters of the other *tzaddikim*, the holy men, were confined to the domestic realms, Edel got to spend her days in the *beit midrash*, the house of study, with her father's disciples, and could argue *halacha* with the best of them. No words were sweeter to her than when her father would say, "Edel is right."

Her mother, Chana, would sometimes encourage her to try to make friends with the other girls in the village, but Edel would roll her eyes and explain that they had nothing in common. What could someone like her, a mystic who had the ear of the great and wise Baal Shem Tov, and had been his sole companion on his latest pilgrimage to the Holy Land—what could she possibly discuss with girls who spent their days sewing and baking bread? Her mother didn't even read Hebrew, so what could she possibly understand about the mysteries of the universe and her father's divine mission?

Though the Baal Shem Tov's most recent attempt to reach the Holy Land had ended in disaster and near starvation in Istanbul, accompanying her father on his mission had invigorated Edel, and she eagerly awaited the next chapter in their lives of prophecy and adventure. She was crestfallen to discover that his latest mission for her was not spiritual, but domestic. He informed her that a marriage proposal for her had been made by Rabbi Yekiel Ashkenazi. He had sent a disciple to test the young man's Torah knowledge, and Edel wondered why she could not perform the test herself. Still, she loved her father and trusted that he would only agree to marry her to someone worthy.

Rabbi Yekiel was agreeable enough, but once they were married, Edel found he had taken her place at the Baal Shem Tov's side. Now her father asked Yekiel to accompany him on his journeys, not Edel. And to her horror, Edel found her life confined to that of the domestic women, whose company she had always dreaded. She maintained her studies as best she could when the housekeeping was done for the day, even though her aching back made it hard to concentrate. Her one solace was that the Baal Shem Tov trusted her with his *Book of Remedies*, and she got to serve as a healer while he was away.

Once she managed to find time to slip into the beit midrash, but she no longer knew the students, and this latest crop was unfamiliar with her and gave her strange looks. While she used to find their debates thrilling, now she found these young men tiresome and moronic. Even when the Baal Shem Tov praised her correct answer and said "Edel is right," it felt like a pat on the head one gives a dog who does a trick.

Feeling bereft, Edel tried to make peace with her role, even if that meant she felt she would never belong. It seemed her destiny was not to be her father's successor, but to give birth to the next successor.

Then one day she was summoned to the house of a child who needed healing and was surprised when his mother quoted the *Gemara*. The woman explained that her father had been a *tzaddik*, a learned man, and used to study with her until she got married. Edel was at once crestfallen to discover she wasn't the only girl who was knowledgeable in Torah but also thrilled to meet a kindred spirit. Edel wondered how many others there could be and why she hadn't met them.

That night, Edel had a vision. She imagined herself in a beit midrash—but unlike any that her father had convened. This one was full of light and color, and the students weren't just pockmarked young men, but also women. Not only that, but these women were wearing *kippot* and *tzit-tzit,* fringes on the corners of their garments. There were also men wearing flowing frocks, and others whose gender she could not determine, who flitted about the room in sheer wings, advising on Aramaic grammar. She accidentally bumped into one of the winged ones, who invited her to sit.

She said to the one with wings, "How wonderful it is that the Jewish world has finally transformed—so everyone has equal opportunity to be Torah scholars."

The person with wings laughed and said, "I wish. But we're a pretty small sliver of the Jewish world. And there are still plenty of people who don't think we have the right to do what we do."

Edel asked, "Then why do this?"

"Well, we may not be able to change the whole world, but if we change enough individual worlds, and they go on to change the worlds around them ... who knows where that could lead?"

Edel woke from her dream, buzzing with prophecy. Her vision was tantalizing but also discouraging. On the one hand, the future would indeed be slightly more open, but not nearly enough.

Later that day, the woman she'd met the day before came to pick up more remedy for her son. As she turned to leave, Edel asked, "Would you like to stay for tea and discuss some Torah?" And discuss some Torah they did.

It may not have looked or sounded like the Torah debated at length in the beit midrash. Its commentaries may have faded into the sands of time. But these women did exist, along with countless versions of them and others whose dress, orientation, and appearance would make them unworthy of being recorded by the old men in their record books. Despite being unnamed, unacknowledged, and unordained, these unconventional scholars have lit countless sparks across time, waiting to be kindled by those ready to blaze the trails for change.

ABOUT THE STORY

This story is adapted from several stories in *The Light and Fire of the Baal Shem Tov* by Yitzhak Buxbaum. The story of the Baal Shem Tov's only daughter, Edel, really captivated me when I encountered her, and yet I was also frustrated that her story seemed to end after she got married. Like so many brilliant women in Jewish text and history, she seems to exist in isolation—the exception in a world where women cannot learn on the same level as men. Rarely do these women ever get the chance to share wisdom and learn from each other. Edel's story also resonated with me as someone happily raised as a girl in my dad's world of Jewish thought and humor, only to grow older and realize that as a woman, I was subject to very different standards and expectations. The beit midrash with the fairy wings at the end of the story is an homage to SVARA: A Radically Queer Yeshiva, which has helped me, and other marginalized people, have access to deep Jewish learning.

A Woman and a Sultan

JOSÉ DE KWAADSTENIET

It was winter. A Jewish peasant woman was washing sheep's wool in the ice-cold water of a stream. She washed, and she washed: dipping, pulling. She shivered, and her fingers felt like ice.

Just then, the sultan of that region strode along the stream and saw the woman. He watched her for a moment, walked up to her, taking care that he didn't get his beautiful clothes dirty, and then asked her, out of the blue, "Tell me, does five exceed seven?"

The woman looked up at the sultan and shrugged. "Let me ask you a question. Does twelve exceed thirty-two?"

The retinue of the sultan (a sultan has an entourage, of course) looked at each other, their eyes wide and wondering—what on earth was going on here?

"Was your house ever on fire?" the sultan asked.

"Just one fire? Ah! We already had six, and still one more to come," the woman answered.

By now, the sultan's entourage was speechless: how could these two understand each other so perfectly? What was more: how could they make heads or tails of these mysterious riddles?

The sultan had another question. "Now, suppose I send you one of my pigeons. Are you capable of plucking him?"

"Ha! Well, send me a pigeon, and we'll find out, won't we?"

The sultan strode on with his entourage, who by now seemed to be very interested in their own feet, no one uttering a word.

Suddenly the sultan asked his chief advisor, "Tell me, did you understand what this conversation I had with the woman was about?"

The chief advisor, lifting up his eyes to heaven, exclaimed, "How could I? You were talking in riddles!"

The sultan bellowed, "Shame on you! A simple Jewish woman understood me perfectly and you, who are supposed to be the wisest man in the country, have no clue! You know what? I give you three days to come up with the answers; if not: you're fired!"

The chief advisor rushed home and summoned all the sages and counselors of the court, but no one could help him. Finally, he sent for the woman to come to the palace and asked her, "Tell me, what was the meaning of the conversation the sultan had with you, of all these questions?"

"If you give me a thousand dinars, I'll tell you."

"A thousand dinars?! For just a few words? You've got a nerve!"

"Take it or leave it. Whatever. It's fine by me," she said and went home.

The third day came, and the chief advisor sent for the woman again. "Here." He handed her a sack. "You've got your thousand dinars. Tell me the answers!"

She tucked away the money safely under her clothes and started to explain. "The sultan saw me washing the wool in the ice-cold water, and he asked me, 'Does five exceed seven?' What he meant was: were you not able to earn your money for the whole year during spring and summer, that you also have to work during these five cold months?

"I answered him, 'Does twelve exceed thirty-two?' meaning: my thirty-two teeth need more to chew on than I can earn in a year.'

"Then the sultan asked, 'Was your house ever on fire?' I answered, 'Already six times, and still one more to come.' Which means we, my husband and I, married off six of our children and, as anybody knows, after a wedding a father and a mother are as broke as after a fire.

"Finally, he asked, 'Suppose I send you one of my pigeons. Are you capable of plucking him?' I said, 'Send me a pigeon, and we'll find out, won't we.' And he sent you. Thank you for the thousand dinars, by the way. Now, I suggest that you go back to the sultan and tell him whether I succeeded—plucking the pigeon, that is."

A sultan and a "simple" Jewish woman—may we all understand each other on such a deep, deep level, and help each other in the process.

ABOUT THE STORY

This story is one of the gems I adapted from Nathan Ausubel's collection, *A Treasury of Jewish Folklore*: *The Stories, Traditions, Legends, Humor, Wisdom and Folk Songs of the Jewish People*. I love the fact that the Jewish peasant woman and the sultan understand each other perfectly. Two people from different worlds, from different social backgrounds, have no trouble at all in this respect. And in a subtle way, the sultan helps the woman to overcome her poverty. Oh, by the way, the Jewish peasant in Ausubel's book was not a woman.

Secret of the Chanukah Flame

DEBRA GORDON ZASLOW

LONG AGO, in the Middle East, there lived a wise Jewish woman called Chava who was a scholar and a beloved healer. When the queen of the realm heard of this wise woman, she was eager to meet her and arranged for her to come to the palace. The queen was so impressed with Chava's wit and kindness that she appointed her to be her personal advisor. Over time, Chava and the queen became fast friends. Not only would Chava advise the queen in the palace, but the queen would also visit Chava at her home.

Once, on the last night of Chanukah, the queen came for a visit. Chava's whole family sat around the table eating potato pancakes and playing dreidel while the candles burned in the eight-branched menorah, the *chanukiah*. The family welcomed the queen and invited her to sit with them. They taught her to spin the dreidel and showed her the letters nun, gimel, hey, and shin. They explained the meaning of the words *nes, gadol, haya, sham*: "A great miracle happened there."

The queen asked, "What miracle?"

Chava told the queen how a small band of freedom fighters, the Maccabees, fought against the Syrian king, Antiochus, and his armies. Then she explained how the Jews came to their ransacked Temple in Jerusalem and then rededicated it with new holy oil.

"The miracle was the miracle of new hope, when a tiny bit of oil kept burning for eight days."

The queen looked slowly around the room until her eyes focused on the chanukiah. She asked, "But why are there so many candles?"

Chava said, "There are eight candles since the oil burned for eight days. We light one more candle for each night of Chanukah until all eight candles are lit."

The queen peered at the chanukiah, counting the candles. "But why is there a ninth candle higher than the rest?"

Chava answered, "That candle is the helper we use to light the other candles, called the *shammash*."

But the queen shook her head. "I don't understand," she said. "There must be a hidden meaning to the shammash, or else why would you keep that one lit, and why on an upper level?"

Chava answered, "I don't know about a hidden meaning."

The queen narrowed her eyes. "Is there a secret that you can't tell me that is shared only among the Jews?"

Before Chava could reply, the queen said, "Three days from now I want you to come to the palace and tell me the truth of the secret of the shammash." With these words, she stood up, said goodnight, and strode out of the house.

What could Chava do? She had no idea what to tell the queen about the secret of the shammash since she didn't know. She had studied all of the Talmud, but she'd never heard of any secret. Should she invent something to please the queen? She puzzled over what to do for the next two days.

On the evening of the second day, she went for a walk outside her house to get some fresh air. As she strolled down the street, past neighborhood houses, she felt the quiet of the night. Suddenly she sensed a presence and noticed an old woman walking beside her whom she hadn't seen before. They walked together quietly until the old woman spoke. "Well, Chava, who is going to carry whom?"

Chava peered at the old woman, wondering if she was in her right mind. She thought, *Perhaps I'm strong enough to carry you, but you are way too feeble to carry me.* Chava said nothing, and they continued to walk in silence.

After they passed a faded gray house, they heard the sound of weeping coming from inside. When they saw a coffin near the door, they knew someone had died.

The old woman turned to Chava and asked, "Is the person in the coffin dead or alive?" Now Chava was sure the old woman was disoriented and decided not to reply.

As they continued walking, they passed a field. The old woman said, "Look at those ears of wheat! I wonder if they've been eaten yet." Chava just shook her head.

Eventually, they walked back toward Chava's house. As they approached the house, the old woman said, "I wonder if there are living creatures in this pleasant home."

Chava laughed and said, "This house is my house. Why don't you come in and have a cup of tea, and we'll see if the people in it are living?"

The old woman came in, sat down, and took a cup of tea. Chava turned to her and said, "Now, please tell me. Why did you ask if there were living creatures in this house?"

The old woman replied, "By living creatures, I meant children. When children are raised with love of the Torah, then they can keep their joy of life always."

Chava said, "There are indeed children here who love the Torah, but they are sleeping now." She realized the woman was not crazy, but speaking in riddles to make some kind of sense, so she asked, "And what were you talking about when you asked if the wheat in the field had already been eaten?"

The old woman replied, "I wondered if the people who planted the field had debts they'd have to pay with the crop. In that case, the crop would be someone else's before it was picked."

"Ah," Chava said and smiled. "I see what you mean. But what about the question of the person in the coffin being alive or dead?"

The old woman answered, "Well, when a person lives by the

Torah and does *mitzvot*, their acts of lovingkindness live on after them. When their body is gone, their soul remains and goes on living eternally."

Now Chava was sure the woman was very clever. "Tell me, what did you mean when you asked who should carry whom? I could not make sense of that."

The old woman smiled and answered, "When people walk together, they tell stories, sing songs, or have a discussion. This makes traveling easier, as though one person were holding up the other. So what I was asking was, who will be the first to bring up something interesting to lighten the journey?"

Chava said, "Well, you have certainly told me some very interesting things." And they sat quietly for a while. Then the old woman leaned over and said, "I can see that something is troubling you deeply."

Chava felt this woman might understand, so she told her about the queen's visit and her demand to come and reveal the secret of the shammash. "I tried to explain it to the queen, but she accused me of keeping something from her. What can I say tomorrow? Does the shammash have a secret?"

The old woman sat for a while with her eyes half-closed, as if contemplating the question. Then she said, "Tell the queen that this is the hidden meaning: The shammash stands up high above the others to declare: 'Everyone look up toward my light. I represent the first, primal light of creation, the light that constantly ignites sparks everywhere.'"

The old woman continued, "We are all like candles. Each of us is a holy spark of the divine, and even in the darkest times, we can be reignited by the light of creation within us. And, like the shammash, we must see the light of creation in ourselves and let it be a spark that ignites others. We must always share our divine light with the world."

As Chava listened, tears streamed down her face.

She turned to thank the old woman, but she had vanished into the night. Chava thought, *Could it be that the mysterious visitor was none other than Serach bat-Asher, the ancient prophetess?* Her heart was filled with gratitude and awe.

The next day at the palace, the queen rose to greet Chava eagerly. "You have come right on time," she said. "Will you tell me the secret now?"

Chava said, "I will share the secret with you."

She told the queen what Serach bat-Asher had told her. "The shammash stands above to remind us of the first light of creation, the highest light, that ignites the divine sparks in all of us."

The queen's eyes were wide. "Who taught you this?" she asked.

"A special visitor came to me," said Chava. She ignited a spark in me, to share with you, just like the shammash lights the candles.

The queen drew in her breath and closed her eyes. "Of course," she said. "The first light of creation is inside us all, always reigniting. As queen, I try to ignite sparks of inspiration in my people. Now I see. Thank you for sharing that spark with me."

So, the two of them continued their long friendship, always igniting the sparks of the divine in each other. And so may we all see the light in each other, and share our sparks, especially in times of darkness.

ABOUT THE STORY

This is adapted from Peninnah Schram's story, "The Secret of the Shammash," in *Eight Tales for Eight Nights: Stories for Chanukah* by Peninnah Schram and Steven M. Rosman. It is based on a story by Nissan Mindel in *Talks and Tales,* edited by N. Mindel. Peninnah Schram gave permission for my version that substitutes a queen and a wise woman for the male characters. On Peninnah's suggestion, I invited Serach bat-Asher to stand in for Elijah.

The substance of the story remains intact, except

for the secret revealed at the end. Although I like the original revelation, I resonate more with the idea of the shammash being the first light that sparks the light of creation in us all.

Hannah and the Moon

GAIL PASTERNACK

Deep in the heart of Eastern Europe, there was once a village called Chelm. Many considered it a village of fools, but the Chelmites knew they were wise, even if their wisdom looked a little different from everyone else's. They were a curious people who liked to ask scholarly questions, especially Hannah, the milkmaid.

Hannah asked many questions. She couldn't help herself. Every day she saw wondrous things that she needed to understand.

One day she got up early in the morning to milk her cows, and as she walked to the barn, her feet got wet from the dew on the grass. But later that day, when she delivered milk and cheese, the grass was dry.

"Where does dew come from?" she asked Freyde, the woman who worked at the butcher shop. "And where does it go?"

"It comes from the tears of the moon," Freyde said. "On nights, when it gets too cold for the moon to warm itself, the moon gets sad, and it cries. But during the day, when the sun gets too warm, it drinks up the dew to cool itself."

Of course, Hannah thought. Freyde was truly the wisest woman in the village.

Hannah went home, appreciating the warmth of the sun on her

for the secret revealed at the end. Although I like the original revelation, I resonate more with the idea of the shammash being the first light that sparks the light of creation in us all.

Hannah and the Moon

GAIL PASTERNACK

Deep in the heart of Eastern Europe, there was once a village called Chelm. Many considered it a village of fools, but the Chelmites knew they were wise, even if their wisdom looked a little different from everyone else's. They were a curious people who liked to ask scholarly questions, especially Hannah, the milkmaid.

Hannah asked many questions. She couldn't help herself. Every day she saw wondrous things that she needed to understand.

One day she got up early in the morning to milk her cows, and as she walked to the barn, her feet got wet from the dew on the grass. But later that day, when she delivered milk and cheese, the grass was dry.

"Where does dew come from?" she asked Freyde, the woman who worked at the butcher shop. "And where does it go?"

"It comes from the tears of the moon," Freyde said. "On nights, when it gets too cold for the moon to warm itself, the moon gets sad, and it cries. But during the day, when the sun gets too warm, it drinks up the dew to cool itself."

Of course, Hannah thought. Freyde was truly the wisest woman in the village.

Hannah went home, appreciating the warmth of the sun on her

skin. But the cool of the night was lovely too. All night she thought about the sun and moon, unable to decide which she liked best.

The next day, she asked Freyde, "What is more important, the sun or the moon?"

"The moon, of course!" Freyde said. "It shines at night, when it is needed. The sun—pfft. It shines only during the day when it's already light."

After that revelation, Hannah gazed up at the sky every night, and the more she did, the more baffled she became. *How strange*, she thought. The moon always changed—getting big and full one night and then disappearing altogether several weeks later. And oh, those nights when it disappeared. So dark. Hannah couldn't see her own hands, and she often would trip over her neighbor's goat when she went for a walk in the evening.

Several weeks later, Hannah visited her cousin in another town. When she took her evening stroll, she saw the most astonishing thing. On every street corner there were poles with glowing globes of light on top of them. They were like mini moons on every street corner!

When Hannah went back to Chelm, she convinced the elders to call a council meeting. Everyone in Chelm came.

"Chelm needs these lamps in the street," Hannah said.

"We do!" Rachel, the lacemaker said.

Freyde agreed. So did Leeba, the watercarrier.

But the elders of Chelm scratched their chins and shook their heads.

The wisest elder stood. "Where will we get the money for these lights on the street? We can't take it from the fund to feed the poor. We can't take it from our schools."

The Chelmites murmured in agreement. "We cannot afford these lamps," they all said.

Hannah thought and thought until she had the most brilliant idea. "I've got it," she said. "We'll steal the moon! Then we can use it whenever we need it." And she told them her plan of how they could do it.

The next day they set to work. Young and old went to the forest to fetch wood to bring to Yosele the barrel maker, and Yosele made the biggest barrel he had ever made. It was so tall that the villagers needed to stand on step stools so they could see inside it. And it was so wide that all the Chelmites could stand shoulder-to-shoulder in a circle around it. When Yosele was done, it took ten Chelmites to drag the barrel to the village center.

Leeba organized a group of villagers to help her bring water from the river. They filled the barrel with water, up to the very rim. Hannah collected scrap fabrics from each household, and Rachel invited all the village women to her house to sew the fabric into a cover for the barrel.

Every night the Chelmites watched the moon. It started as a crescent, but it grew and grew until finally one night it was big and full. The villagers clustered around the barrel. Mothers and fathers put children on their shoulders so they could see. Everyone peered into the barrel.

They watched the moon slowly immerse itself in the water. At first, just a small sliver glowed on the surface, but then they saw more and more until the entire moon shone bright in the barrel. Rachel and Hannah unfolded the huge cover the women had made, and with the help of other villagers, they spread it over the top of the barrel and pulled it taut. Freyde and Leeba encircled the barrel to wrap a rope around the edges of the fabric. They then yanked on the rope and tied it tight.

The Chelmites were so busy covering the barrel, they didn't notice that clouds had rolled in and blanketed the sky. When they looked up and saw no moon, they were certain that they had safely trapped it in their barrel. It got dark without a moon, yet there was enough light for the villagers to get home safely.

Clouds covered the sky every night that month. No one saw a bit of the moon, but the villagers did notice that the nights got darker and darker until one night, it was pitch black out.

They returned to the barrel and uncovered it, certain that the light of the moon would fill the sky. But when all the Chelmites peered into the barrel—nothing! No moon.

"Where did it go?" Rachel asked.

Hannah thought. "I know. It must have escaped and snuck away when no one was looking. We should try this again next month and have guards watching day and night."

"What a wonderful idea," Freyde said.

And all the Chelmites agreed. They went to bed that night confident that Hannah's new plan would work.

I know what you're thinking. That plan won't work either. No one can steal the moon! And yet, I think we can learn from the Chelmites. We all come up against obstacles in our daily lives, but we don't need to face them alone. Instead, we can unite with our family and friends, and like the Chelmites, help each other. Together we can overcome our challenges and achieve some truly wondrous things.

ABOUT THE STORY

Jewish storytellers have told Chelm stories for over a hundred years. These stories may have originated from a 1597 collection of German comic stories called *Schildburg Tales*, which were translated into Yiddish in the eighteenth century. In 1887, these stories were retold in *Der Khelmer Khokhem*, the first book to place them in the town of Chelm. (An actual town in Poland, but an imaginary one in Jewish folklore.) Versions of this particular story appear in *A Treasury of Yiddish Stories* by Irving Howe and Eliezer Greenberg, *Capturing the Moon* by Edward M. Feinstein, *Rachel the Clever* by Josepha Sherman, *Let's Steal the Moon* by Blanche Luria Serwer, and many other collections. In my version, I highlight how a curious milkmaid inspires the community to come together to do an impossible task.

The Thirty-Sixth Night of Chanukah

CASSANDRA SAGAN

Our story begins in the heart of Jewish magical realism, the village of Chelm, where the souls of harmless fools had fallen from the beaks of birds, and a little feather landed in each of our hearts. No one ever left Chelm—why would they? But many people passed through: merchants and wanderers, mystics and outcasts. Every traveler eventually declared, "You people are fools!"

Mitzi the baker smiled and said, "You are making me blush with your compliments!"

The grocer said, "My friend, you are too kind."

Golde the Mayor turned to the gathered crowd and declared, "May our foolishness be a light unto the nations!"

But Zelda Nudelman said, "Hmmmph. I'm no fool!"

And then there was the time when a caravan of visitors brought with them an airborne virus, and a pandemic spread rapidly through the village. Shops were closed, masks were sewn, and everyone began to shelter in place and work from home.

Zelda already had an extra table in the kitchen where she hummed to herself while crafting *tchotchke* jewelry: little hamantaschen for Purim and dreidel pendants for Chanukkah. Zelda once created a *sukkah* small enough for hummingbirds, and she even made prayer shawls for stuffed animals.

Her husband, Shmoo, was a tailor, a kindly but extremely messy man. All the village shops closed by order of the mayor, so he had to throw all of his supplies into a wagon and schlep them home. Thus, the Nudelman cottage overflowed with rolls and scraps of fabric, broken sewing machines, oily spare parts, piles of thimbles, clippings, shears with their sharp mouths opened like Leviathans, patterns, buttons, and spools of thread unspooling. He kissed her with a mouthful of pins until she looked like a voodoo doll, and occasionally he rolled across the room on loose spools of thread as if they were wheels.

The pandemic dragged on for many months, and poor Zelda, who thrived in a clean and orderly home, began having a hard time. She left the shells on the sunflower seeds when she baked challah. She used schmaltz to clean the floors. One time she filled her *kreplach* dumplings with pickled herring.

As Chanukah approached, Shmoo said, "Zelda, dahlink, it's been a hard year. What can I give you for Chanukah that would make you happy?"

Without a moment's hesitation Zelda said, "I'd like you to clean up the house for all the nights of Chanukah and gift me with living in a tidy house."

After quite a few moments of hesitation, Shmoo smiled. "I will do that for you, my dear." He sealed it with a kiss, and seven pin pricks.

And tidy up he did. Zelda helped, and when everything was scrubbed and rinsed, polished and put in its place, she sighed a deep sigh of relief: aaaaahaaaaahhhaaaaah.

Now, in the town of Chelm they did not celebrate Chanukah the same way that we do. They had read about the ancient argument between Rabbi Hillel and Rabbi Shammai regarding the correct way to light the candles. Shammai said that we should imitate the diminishing light by starting with eight candles and taking one away each night. Hillel said we must always bring in more light, and that we should start with one candle and add one each night. Clearly Hillel won, because we've all done it this way for centuries. But the

Chelmites never heard that the argument had been resolved. So for the sake of fairness, each year they would flip the *chanukiah* (the Chanukah menorah) around, one year lighting Hillel style, and one year lighting the Shammai way.

In this pandemic year, they were lighting Hillel style, adding one new flame each night. At sunset, the Chelmites gathered in front of the shul, masked and standing six feet apart, to sing the blessings and kindle the lights.

Zelda Nudelman had a thought: *why not make Chanukah, and her clean home, last a little longer?* And so, before dawn on the fourth day of Chanukah, Zelda tiptoed over to the synagogue and, using all her strength, turned the chanukiah around to the Shammai direction.

That evening, the townspeople assembled to watch the rabbi light the chanukiah. The rabbi noticed that it was facing the Shammai direction, lifted his eyebrows, shrugged and said, "Why not?" All the Chelmites shrugged and said, "Why not?" They lit the flame and sang the blessings and went home to eat applesauce with a tiny latke on top, as was their custom.

Everyone was happy, and no one more than Zelda in her clean, uncluttered house.

Before dawn of the morning that everyone thought was the eighth night, when only a single flame was to be kindled, Zelda switched up the chanukiah once more so that it was now facing the Hillel orientation. No one seemed to mind, because everyone in Chelm loved Chanukah. The villagers sang their favorite songs, ate sour cream and donut holes, and not a single Chelmite *kvetched* about Chanukah going on for so long because they were in the middle of a pandemic and had kind of lost track of time anyway.

And so Zelda continued basking in her clean home and performing her predawn switcheroos for many weeks, until the thirty-sixth night of Chanukkah.

As the Chelmites gathered in front of the shul, a peddler wandered into the village, and seeing the people of Chelm still lighting the chanukiah in January, he said, "You people are fools! It's almost *Tu B'Shvat*, the New Year of the Trees."

The people of Chelm laughed until their faces were wet with tears. They held their bellies and rolled on the ground. They took off their shoes, as was their custom, and put them on the opposite feet. They danced and jumped for joy.

Zelda lifted her chin and said, "Ha, who's the fool? We have been bringing more light and joy into the world all these weeks. What have you been doing?"

Golde the Mayor said, "If we did something wrong, that is wonderful!" Everyone agreed, nodding vigorously. "We can always learn something from our mistakes, and life is for learning."

The townspeople turned to Mayor Golde and said, "*Nu*, what did we learn?"

Golde tapped on her chin, her forehead, and pulled on her ear, considering. "Next year," she proclaimed, "instead of turning the chanukiah around, I bless us to be the ones who turn ourselves towards light and joy."

When Shmoo returned to work in his village shop, keeping things in order had become second nature. His customers no longer stabbed their stockinged feet on loose pins and scissors, and business grew. And he still helped to keep their home neat and clean.

Said Zelda, "So who's the fool?"

ABOUT THE STORY

According to *The YIVO Encyclopedia of Jews in Eastern Europe*, the first edition of Chelm-like stories indeed appeared in 1597. I imagine that all our stories must pass through the mythical city of Chelm, and the wise foolish women of Chelm deserve to have their voices heard. In that spirit, and from the other side of the pandemic of 2020-23, I created this original story.

PART TWO
Mothers and Daughters

The Mountain and the Cliff

RIVKAH COBURN

ONCE UPON a time, in a little village in the Old Country, which was sometimes in Poland and sometimes in Ukraine, there lived a mother and her daughter. The mother was a merchant who made a very modest living selling a little bit of this and a little bit of that to the people in the village. Once a month, Penina and her daughter, Rivkelah, would load up their wagon and hitch up their horse to ride to other villages and sell a little bit of this and a little bit of that to the people who lived there.

The village that Penina and Rivkelah lived in was in a beautiful valley surrounded by mountains with only one road leading out of the village. The only way to get to the neighboring towns was to take the one road and cross the mountain range as it wound its way up to the tallest mountain. For Rivkelah, this was an exciting journey!

One spring day, Rivkelah and her mother loaded up their wagon with a little bit of this and a little bit of that. With a shake of the reins, the horse began to lead them out of their village and onto their big adventure. Soon, the horse and wagon began to climb its way up the narrow road, through the twists and turns, toward the top of the mountain.

They were almost at the top of the mountain when they came around a curve. The horse suddenly stopped. There, in the middle of the road, was a huge pile of rocks. To one side was the mountain, and to the other, a steep cliff. There was nowhere for them to go. They would have to turn around and go back home.

As Penina began to get up from her seat, Rivkelah grabbed her mother's hands and said, "Don't worry *Ima*, you stay here. I'll get rid of those rocks and then we'll be on our way."

Rivkelah bounded down from the wagon and ran to the huge rock pile. She began to push the rocks, pull the rocks, throw the rocks, and roll the rocks over the cliff with great joy. Her mother sat with a quiet smile on her face and watched as her strong-willed daughter removed what stood in their way.

Rivkelah worked for several hours as the sun moved across the sky. Her arms ached, and sweat dripped into her eyes. Finally, all the rocks were cleared, except for one.

The rock that remained was the largest and the heaviest. And it was right in the middle of the road! The horse and wagon could not go around it with the mountain to one side and the cliff on the other side.

With bleary eyes and a heavy heart, Rivkelah slowly walked back to the wagon and said, "I'm sorry, Ima, I can't move the last rock. We have to turn around and go home after all."

Penina looked at her daughter and asked, "Are you sure you have done everything you can do to move the rock?"

Rivkelah thought for a moment, then her eyes brightened. She ran to the back of the wagon and reached into a bag that had a little bit of this and a little bit of that and pulled out a large piece of fabric. She wrapped the fabric around the rock, tied the ends together, and pulled on it with all her might. The rock didn't budge. Panting, she went back to the wagon. "Ima, it didn't work. We're going to have to go home."

Penina again asked, "Are you sure you have done everything you can do?"

Rivkelah thought again. She ran back to the wagon that held a little bit of this and a little bit of that and pulled out a long board that she quickly wedged under the large rock. Rivkelah pushed and pushed and then jumped on it with all her might. The rock still stayed put. Dragging her spirits, along with the board, back to the wagon, Rivkelah said to her mother, "Ima, it's no use. I give up. We have to go back."

Once again Penina asked, "Are you sure you have done *everything* you can do?"

This time Rivkelah burst out in anger, "Yes! Yes! I am sure I have done everything I can do! I have pulled the rock. I have pushed the rock. I have jumped on the board to move the rock. But it won't budge! I have done everything possible, Ima!"

Penina shook her head and gently said, "No, Rivkelah, you haven't done everything. You haven't asked me to help you."

Rivkelah brushed away her tears as her mother got down from the wagon. Together, mother and daughter crouched down shoulder to shoulder. Together they gripped the rock. Together they grunted and heaved and shoved with all their might. And then together, they slowly rolled that huge rock, inch by inch, right off the cliff.

Then, together, they climbed back onto the wagon and, with a shake of the reins, they were on their way to sell a little bit of this and a little bit of that.

ABOUT THE STORY

I first encountered a version of this story told by Rabbi David Holtz in Peninnah Schram's *Chosen Tales, Stories Told by Jewish Storytellers*. Throughout the years, "The Mountain and the Cliff" became one of my signature stories. As a dancer, I delighted in physically embodying the story as I told it. At one point, in my telling of the story, two female characters took the place of the two male characters. It was a natural shift that resonated with me as a woman wanting to empower other women in non-stereotypical roles. Adapted with permission from Rabbi David Holtz.

The Little Magpie

LISA HUBERMAN

Rokhl knew her mother was frustrated with her. No matter how hard she tried, Rokhl could not stop herself from accumulating odds and ends wherever she went—fallen buttons, ornate drawer knobs, bits of fabric scraps. If there was a pile of trash, her eyes would immediately zoom in on the glint of light shining off a broken clock face or the golden brocade thread of a ripped jacket.

Di kleine magpie—everyone in the village called her. The little magpie.

Not only did Rokhl have an eye for beautiful, discarded things, but she also had a knack for reinventing them. If someone complimented her on a new broach or charm bracelet, she would proudly recite the provenance of each part. "Why, thank you! Would you believe this actually used to be part of the inside of a pocket watch? And this was the buckle of a shoe my brother couldn't wear anymore. And this one …"

While it was a sweet quirk when she was young, as she grew older, people called her di kleine magpie in a less affectionate way. Her father would buy Rokhl beautiful new dresses and shawls to wear to shul, and instead she would prefer to wear the worn clothes that she patchworked herself from old curtains, handkerchiefs, or tablecloths she'd found. As the congregation giggled and stared, her mother fretted. *They must all think we are too poor to dress her properly*!

Though Rokhl's outward appearance would make it difficult for her to find a good match for a husband, her mother still hoped—and tried to equip her daughter with some knowledge of basic housekeeping. But whether it was sewing, cooking, or laundry, Rokhl was always lost in her own thoughts.

One Friday afternoon, Rokhl's mother was walking her through preparation of Shabbat dinner for the matchmaker. It was an elaborate dance involving the exact timing of chopping vegetables, boiling chicken, and baking bread before sundown. All required adherence to a precise set of instructions and choreography—but Rokhl seemed much more focused on something she was fidgeting with in her pocket.

To snap her back into reality, her mother clapped her hands in her daughter's face. "Rokhl! Do you hear a word I am saying?"

Rokhl seemed completely unbothered and instead proudly displayed her latest treasure from her pocket. "Look, Mama! This was a giant tangle, and I have spent the last five hours freeing the pieces. I thought it was just one big chain, but it turns out there were five of them. Isn't that marvelous?"

Her mother pursed her lips while tears trickled down her cheek. Then she drew in her breath. "You know what won't be marvelous? When no one will marry you! When you are so lost in your own thoughts and fantasies that everyone who cares about you—"

Rokhl's mother didn't have time to finish her sentence because the next thing she knew, flames were flying up from the stove and her *babushka*—her kerchief—had caught fire. Rokhl screamed, "Mama!" then grabbed a bucket of water and extinguished the flames. The fire was out, but her mother, and the challah that was rising on the table, were drenched.

For a few moments, the two stood in silence. Rokhl grabbed a cloth and attempted to pat her mother down, but the older woman waved her away and said, "Just go to your room and stay there until *Shabbos*. I'll finish this myself."

Rokhl nodded, went upstairs to her room, and began to weep. She knew she had disappointed her mother—was always disappointing her mother. She had always been too strange, too messy, too unfocused. She earnestly tried to be good—to only focus on the current moment and the simple tasks she was given. But tasks that seemed easy for those like her mother were terrifying for her. Running her hands across a shiny piece of discarded silver or porcelain would sometimes be the only thing that soothed her enough to keep her from fleeing.

Shabbos was still two hours away, and Rokhl grew restless. She attempted to focus on one of her ongoing repair projects, a torn sweater that she was embroidering with flowers to cover some holes. She was making progress, but something was missing. Though her mother had commanded her to stay in her room, Rokhl found herself unable to remain still.

She quietly stepped out into the hallway, hoping inspiration would strike. She walked into the sitting room, and her eyes fell on a chest that was tucked way back into the corner, almost as if it were hidden. She knelt down, lifted the cover, and her eyes went wide.

Inside she found an array of treasures: old children's toys, a set of marbles, a small boy's cap. But what drew her eye was a tallit case for a prayer shawl, with ornate blue-and-gold embroidery, and edges scorched by fire. She picked up the tallit case and carried it back to her room—this was the missing element.

She spent the next hour until Shabbos attaching part of the tallit case to the collar of her sweater. Though she knew her mother would hate it, she was proud of her work and wanted to show it off.

The matchmaker arrived along with Rokhl's father. As her mother was still in the kitchen, Rokhl greeted them at the door with as proper courtesy as she could muster and said, "Good Shabbos."

The matchmaker surveyed Rokhl's appearance, noted her sweater, and said, "I see di kleine magpie continues to live up to her name."

Rokhl flushed with both embarrassment and pride and ushered

the party to the table. As they sat down, her mother entered carrying the covered challah and said, "Welcome to our home. I apologize for not having the table fully prepared before you arrived, but I had some delays …"

Rokhl's mother stopped mid-sentence, and her eyes fell on Rokhl. "That sweater."

Rokhl explained, "I know, Mother. You had a different frock picked out for me, but I found the most perfect trim for the collar to complete this one, and I think it just brings everything together, and I'm truly proud of it—"

But her mother slammed the challah on the table. "You know what?" she interrupted. "I have done my best, and you insist on being defiant, on caring more for your … scraps, your trinkets, than your reputation, your family, than anything else in this world. And I give up!" Then she stormed out of the room.

The entire table went silent. Rokhl turned to her father. "I am sorry, Papa. I know you wanted me to make a good match, but I decided it was better to make a match as the girl that I am rather than someone else."

Her father waved his hand. "Your mother was probably just anxious about the dinner."

The matchmaker leaned in closer to examine Rokhl's sweater. "That embroidery is truly extraordinary along the collar. Your skills have improved."

Rokhl shook her head. "Oh, I didn't do that myself. It was part of an old tallit case I found in a chest in the sitting room."

Her father said, "The chest with your uncle's old things?"

Rokhl looked confused. "My uncle?"

A light lit up in the matchmaker's eyes. "Of course! Yossi! Your mother's brother. He perished in that fire—horrible, just horrible."

Rokhl rose from the table. "Excuse me, I'm going to go check on my mother."

Rokhl entered the kitchen and found her mother bent over the soup pot, stirring furiously. She put her hand on her mother's shoulder. "You never told me about Yossi."

Her mother turned and fingered the collar of Rokhl's sweater. "Your grandmother stitched this tallit case for him. She and Yossi were like you—silly, mischievous, always lost together in a world I couldn't enter. Once Father died, it was up to me to keep them safe."

Rokhl said, "The matchmaker said there was a fire …"

Her mother continued, "I was only gone for a few minutes to retrieve water from the well, but your grandmother had knocked over a candlestick. My brother, Yossi, was studying for his bar mitzvah and was so deep in prayer that he didn't notice the smoke until it was too late."

"Oh, Mama," Rokhl said.

The older woman wept. "I couldn't save them, but I thought if I could keep you tethered to this world … but it seems I lost you anyway. And now I'm the one who has ruined your chances of a good match by making a scene at this dinner. Can you forgive me?"

Rokhl embraced her mother. "Of course. And if she never finds me a husband, you'll be stuck with me forever."

Her mother kissed her forehead. "It would be my greatest honor."

Mother and daughter returned to the table, and though the meal was simple, somehow the bread and soup tasted richer than anyone had ever tasted before.

ABOUT THE STORY

I have always been a collector—I blame Ariel from *The Little Mermaid* for making hoarding shiny human trash seem so exotic and appealing. During the pandemic, I got into the culture of "stooping" in New York City—people leave out boxes of treasures they no longer have use for in the hopes that someone will be able to give it a new life. I also became captivated by collecting broken ceramics and sea glass from the Hudson River, sometimes using it to make upcycled jewelry, sometimes just rubbing my fingers over the edges as a source of sensory comfort. Someone recently told me about the kabbalistic concept of *Shevirat haKeilim*, the shattering of vessels at the beginning of the world and human beings' eternal and unending quest to restore them. Perhaps in some ways, that is what those of us are seeking when we see divinity in discarded, broken things. That thought inspired me to write this original story.

Journey of the Lost Princess

DEBRA GORDON ZASLOW

ONCE THERE was a queen who had an only child, a daughter, whom she adored. They would spend time together every day, playing, laughing, and telling stories. The queen would delight the princess with stories of witches, fairies, demons, and dragons.

The princess's favorite story was of a brother and sister who each had a *shofar* from the head of the same ram. When one of them would blow their shofar, the other shofar would vibrate and hum. The princess would beg the queen, "Tell me the shofar story!" and almost no matter what she was doing, the queen would stop and tell that story.

One night, the two of them were riding home from an occasion in the royal carriage on a narrow, winding road on the edge of a steep ravine. Suddenly the wind began to blow, and the carriage shook. It began to rain, thunder clapped, and lightning streaked through the sky. When the horses bolted, the chariot toppled over, and the princess and the queen were thrown out. The queen landed not far away and was knocked unconscious, but the princess tumbled all the way over the cliff into the steep ravine.

The next day, when the queen woke in her bed, she demanded to know where her daughter was. When she was told the princess hadn't been found, she cried, "You must find my daughter—comb the forest, search the ravine, send all my men! Don't come back until you've found her!"

The soldiers went out, but the ground was slick and muddy from the rain, and they couldn't find any tracks. They searched for days but found no trace of the princess. Finally, they returned and told the queen that the princess must surely be dead. Needless to say, the queen was heartbroken. She shut herself in her chambers and refused to speak to anyone.

But the princess was not dead. She had fallen into a crevice between two rocks, where she lay unconscious for three days. When she woke, she looked around but didn't know where she was. She pulled herself out of the crevice and found she was stiff, sore, bleeding, and hungry. She walked through the forest all day, crying pitifully, looking for any sign of something familiar.

At the end of the day, she found a little cave that she crawled into and cried herself to sleep. When she woke, she was staring into the faces of a band of thieves.

"Look, it's a little girl! Who is she? She looks hurt!" They shouted at her, "Who are you? Where do you come from?" But the princess could only stare at them and cry. She couldn't remember who she was or where she came from.

The thieves took pity on her, took her in, and nursed her back to health. After a while, they raised her as one of their own and grew to love her. She was clever and strong and entertained them with all kinds of stories—tales of witches and demons and dragons and fairies. When they asked, "Where did you learn all of these stories?" the princess could not remember. They'd take her with them into the marketplace, where she'd charm the shopkeepers, telling them stories, while the thieves stuffed their pockets with fruits and vegetables and all kinds of trinkets.

Sometimes the princess would ask, "Is this the only way to live? Do we have to steal?" They would answer, "This is the way we know to make a living. It's not good enough for you?" So the princess stopped asking.

One day, while the princess was out walking, she happened

to see the queen's carriage pass by. Something deep inside of her stirred, and she felt a longing to be in the presence of the queen. She walked all day, until she stood in front of the palace gates, hoping for a glimpse of the queen, but she never saw her.

The queen had not gotten over the loss of her daughter, even though many years had passed. She only went out when necessary, and she rarely spoke. Her advisors tried all kinds of things to cheer her up. They brought in musicians and clowns and jesters, but nothing worked. One advisor remembered that the queen used to love stories, so they decided to hold a storytelling contest. Whomever could tell the best story to entertain the queen would become the royal storyteller and come to live in the palace.

Word traveled fast, and the princess heard about the contest. She was determined to go, so she practiced her best story, a story with witches and demons and fairies. She went into the forest every day, rehearsing the voices of all the characters until she could hardly speak.

Her adopted family laughed at her. "Now you're trying to live in one of your stories! The royal storyteller?" The princess ignored them, and on the first day of the contest, she walked all the way to the palace.

As she stood in line, she could see the queen sitting at the back of the stage. When it was her turn, she walked up, hoping the queen would look up, but she was slumped in her chair, staring at the floor. The princess's heart beat faster and faster as she opened her mouth and tried to speak. "Once there wa … Once there … Once …" but only a faint croak came out. Someone yelled, "Are you gonna tell a story or not? Get her off the stage!" A guard yelled, "Next!" So, she had to step down.

The next day, she practiced again and arrived even more determined. When it was her turn, she walked up on the stage, cleared her throat, and concentrated with all her might. She took a deep breath and said, "Once …" She cleared her throat and began again. Once there was …" but only a hoarse whisper emerged. She saw the queen look up, and something flickered in her face, but then she slumped over again. The princess tried harder, "Once there was …" but it was inaudible. The people yelled, "Get her off the stage!" Again, the guards called, "Next!" as they led her away.

The next day was the last day of the contest. The princess gathered up all her courage and returned, praying this time her voice would serve her. She waited and walked on stage. Her heart was beating so fast, she felt like she would explode. She began, "Once there was …" but all that came out was a raspy croak. A guard called, "Get her off the stage!"

Then someone else yelled, "I know her! I've seen her with the band of thieves in the marketplace! Grab her!" As the guards ran to seize her, the princess shouted out, "Once there was—" This time her voice rang out at full volume through the crowd.

The queen sat up straight and cried, "Stop! Let her speak!"

The princess spoke slowly, as if faintly reaching for a memory from long ago, while the crowd grew silent. "Once … there … was … a brother and sister … who each had a shofar … from the head of the same ram." Her voice grew stronger as she continued. "When one of them blew their shofar, the other shofar would vibrate and hum. The two of them would play with their shofars, blowing back and forth while moving farther and farther apart.

"One day, when the sister was playing with her friends, she wandered off into the forest just as it was getting dark. Her friends called to her, but she ignored them. She wandered farther away until she realized she was alone in the forest and had no idea how to get back. It was dark and cold, and she knew she'd have to spend the night outside alone. She sat down by a tree and opened her knapsack to see if she had any food, when she saw she had her shofar.

She picked up that shofar and blew a long blast. Far away at home, her brother heard his shofar vibrate and hum. He knew his sister was in trouble, so he picked up his shofar and blew back to her. His sister felt her shofar hum, and she knew she was saved. She blew back to him, and they blew back and forth through the night, until he guided her all the way back home."

When the princess was done telling the story, she looked up

and her eyes met the queen's. The queen rose from her seat. Tears streamed down her face as she stepped down, opened up her arms, and very gently drew her daughter to her heart. She welcomed her back to her true home, the home where she really belonged.

Each year when we hear the sound of the shofar, something stirs deep inside of us and we long to return to our true home, the home of the soul. We cry out to God, "Even if you don't recognize our faces, hear our voices ... Please, hear our voices."

ABOUT THE STORY

Years ago, I decided to create my own story for Rosh Hashanah (Jewish New Year) based on the theme of return. Instead of the usual tale of a prince straying from the king, my version had a lost princess return to the king through the power of storytelling. An earlier version of this story appeared in *Chosen Tales: Stories Told by Jewish Storytellers* edited by Peninnah Schram. In the current version, I completed the feminine transformation by substituting a queen for the king. The story within the story is based on Howard Schwartz's "The Tale of the Shofar" from *The Dream Assembly: Tales of Rabbi Zalman Schachter-Shalomi.*

My Mother's Candlesticks

JOSÉ DE KWAADSTENIET

My Shabbat candlesticks belonged to my mother. That's a simple sentence with a lot of meaning for me. That's what this story is about.

My mother and I were both only children, but our attitude toward that status differed. My mother loved being an only child; I hated it. Basically, I was there to make her happy, which of course was a roadmap heading for disaster. Let's say we had a complicated relationship.

And for the record: I'm from a Christian family.

My mother's candlesticks popped up about thirty years ago. I didn't pay attention because I didn't like them. At a certain point they were just there, on the sideboard in the living room of my parents' apartment, with all the other stuff my mother accumulated. They were still standing there when my mother died in 2013, at age eighty-four.

By then those candlesticks were tarnished, because for a long time my mother was not able to live up to her own standards anymore. Meaning: she couldn't do her own housework, all by herself. Help from outside? Thanks, but no thanks.

In case you might wonder: where was my father? He was sitting on the couch, to the full satisfaction of both of them. So he won't be present in this story? Actually, he will, if you'll have the patience to hear me out.

When my father died some months after my mother, all her jewelry (don't ask) and her silver antiques moved from Rotterdam to our house, in the middle of the country, including the candlesticks. What to do with them? Put them in a cupboard, that's what I did. But somehow, they were not very happy with that location—an accusing vibe was coming from that cupboard. So eventually I took them out, brought them to a jeweler and asked, "Can you tell me where they are from? How old they are? And are they really silver?"

He said, "I will polish them for you and when you come to pick them up, I can tell you more." And a week later he did tell me more. He said, "They are massive silver, and probably English, about a hundred years old. They are worth quite a bit. One piece of advice: don't sell them, at least not now. You won't get enough for them. Better keep them in your cupboard."

And that's what I did. Shining and sparkling, as they were again: back in the cupboard.

Before I proceed with the story, I need to tell you something else.

When I studied theology in the late seventies and early eighties, Professor Rabbi Yehuda Aschkenasy, of blessed memory, made all the difference. He made me realize that Judaism was and is my home—in hindsight, had always been. It took a while, though, before I made the final step by becoming Jewish in 2014, the year the candlesticks started to play their role in my life.

During that summer I had to appear before the *Beit Din* (rabbinical court) of Liberal Judaism in London—one of the progressive branches of Judaism, big in the UK.

Together with a friend who had followed the same path, I arrived in London two days early and, since we had the next day off, we decided to pay a visit to Golders Green, a Jewish neighborhood in London. We wanted to walk around, have a coffee here, a lunch there, visit a synagogue—and of course nose around in Judaica stores.

One of those stores, obviously very Orthodox, was crammed full of books, with everything you might need (or not need) for holidays, with *kippot* (skullcaps), *tallitot* (prayer garments), you name it. And it had a special display case for more valuable objects, like candlesticks.

I looked—and I couldn't believe my eyes. I said to my friend, "Fred, there are my mother's candlesticks!" There they were: the two of them, exactly the same, except they were taller. I said to Fred, "Could it really be that my mother left me two Shabbat candlesticks?"

My Christian mother? True, not very practicing, but still. With her non-Jewish Jewish father, my grandfather.

That needs a little explanation. My dear grandfather always claimed he had a Jewish ancestor. And boy, was he proud of it. Except that ancestor is nowhere to be found. Believe me, I tried.

While I'm at it, a few words about my father, who was obsessed with World War II. It was he who told me, from an early age on, about the *Shoah*, the Holocaust.

My Jewish heritage: my mother's candlesticks, my father's obsession, my grandfather's claim ...

Then came the day of the Beit Din. We went to Leo Baeck College, the educational center of Reform Judaism and Liberal Judaism. When it was my turn—bloody nervous, I can tell you—I entered an impressive, stately chamber of the Manor House, with an equally impressive mantelpiece. The three rabbis sat behind a long table, with their backs to the mantelpiece. And on that impressive mantelpiece, on each corner, stood a candlestick exactly the same as my mother's. Except, again, they were taller. I was speechless, my mind went blank—which didn't last long, thank God, being before the Beit Din.

It all went well. Now, the weird thing was that I was not nervous anymore. And that's not normal, not for me. Nervous, afraid to fail—it is my middle name. So what was going on here? Did my mother help me by showing up in a way that did not, for a change, make me feel uncomfortable?

Two candlesticks on a mantelpiece—on the occasion of my *giur* (conversion to Judaism,) my mother, unknowingly, left me two Shabbat candlesticks.

Back home I found out that the candlesticks are modeled after the two pillars of the Temple of Solomon, named Jachin and Boaz. They still reside in the cupboard most of the week. Except on the seventh day, every Shabbat ever since, they are joyously present: *Blessed are You, Source of blessings, who invites us to bring light to the Shabbat.*

Do I like them now? Honestly, I'm not sure. But I do know that they are dear to me.

So here we are, my mother and me—with my grandfather smiling in the background, and my father nodding. A remarkable and inscrutable case of *l'dor vador*: passing on the tradition from generation to generation.

And you know what? My mother and I are still communicating and understanding each other better as time passes. A process of healing that reaches across the boundary between life and death.

May we all pass on our beautiful tradition and receive it—in every way possible. In every moment possible.

ABOUT THE STORY

This is a story about the remarkable events around my conversion to Judaism, my relationship with my mother (which is a work in progress,) and the mysterious candlesticks that highlight that path.

A Forgiveness Story

DEBRA GORDON ZASLOW

Once a *maggidah*, a wise woman renowned for her stories and profound teachings, was traveling through the countryside when she passed by a small village. The people there had heard of her wisdom, so they asked her to come into their little synagogue and give a talk.

The maggidah said to the congregation, "When an artist paints a picture or a sculptor works with clay, each creation turns out beautiful in its own way, and every piece contains a trace of the artist. It's the same with our creator. God shapes each of us to a special purpose, and we all have a mark of the artist, a spark of the divine. Our deepest work is to recognize that spark in ourselves and each other."

Everyone in the congregation was moved by the maggidah's talk. Outside the synagogue was a deformed beggar, who, because he was ashamed of his hideous appearance, had listened from the window. He was so touched by her words that he decided to ask the maggidah for a personal blessing.

The beggar waited until she came out and walked down the path, and then he emerged. He pulled the shawl from his face and said, "Would you please give me a blessing?"

The maggidah was so startled by the beggar's grotesque face that she blurted out, "God save me from this abomination!"

The beggar growled back, "Oh, an abomination, am I? Did our creator forget the spark of the divine when I was made?"

The maggidah was mortified by what she'd done. She threw herself down at the beggar's feet. She said, "I am so terribly sorry. I don't know what came over me. I've wounded you deeply. Please, can you find it in your heart to forgive me?"

The beggar replied coldly, "I'll forgive you when the one who made me forgives you."

The maggidah threw dirt on herself and began to grovel at the beggar's feet. "I am so deeply sorry," she said. "I cannot leave until I have your forgiveness."

The beggar repeated, "You can leave whenever you like, but I won't forgive you till the one who made me forgives you." The wise woman continued to lie at the beggar's feet while the beggar repeated the same words.

Hours passed. It was getting late, and the maggidah's family was wondering what happened to her. Her children, two sons and a daughter, came looking for their mother and found her lying in the dirt at the feet of the beggar.

The beggar said, "Are you the children of this maggidah? Do you insult people the way she does?"

The oldest son replied, "Oh, our mother would never insult anyone! She's a holy teacher!"

The maggidah looked up and said, "No, it's true. I've offended this man, and I can't leave here until he forgives me."

The oldest son walked up to the beggar and said, "You can see my mother is truly sorry. Please forgive her."

"I'll forgive her when the one who made me forgives her."

Then the second son tried. "Please, have some mercy. Our mother has prostrated herself at your feet. What more can she do?"

"She can do whatever she pleases, but I won't forgive her till the one who made me forgives her."

The rabbi's daughter then walked up to the beggar and very gently took him by the arm. She leaned in close and spoke softly to him.

But before I tell you what she said, I have to tell you what the story said to me.

When I pick a story to tell, there's usually an issue in the story that's calling to me, so I let the story illuminate that issue. It's my way of preparing for the High Holy Days. Obviously, the year I chose this story for Yom Kippur, the issue was forgiveness, particularly self-forgiveness.

I'd been locked in a negative cycle all year, blaming myself for everything. Whenever I came to this place in the story, I knew this was where the story needed to be illuminated. Usually, I meditate on the story and visualize the characters to see what emerges. I kept visualizing and meditating, but nothing was emerging, and High Holy Days were coming up soon.

Sometimes I get inspiration from dreams, so I decided to ask for a dream. I went to bed, using the ancient practice of setting my *kavvanah,* (intention,) and saying a prayer, along with the modern practice of having a notebook, a pen, and a flashlight in case anything came. I felt like I was waiting for the tooth fairy! Nothing came.

By day, the more I meditated on self-forgiveness, the more I realized I was stuck on the issue of parenting. My daughter was experiencing the first pangs of adolescence and was expressing them loudly. Apparently, if you teach your children to express their feelings freely, then eventually they *do*. It was awful. The worst part was, I was blaming myself for all of her pain. In my mind, I was listing the reasons why I had ruined her.

Let's see ...

I weaned her too soon. (She was two and a half.)

Maybe it was the time that I let her cry herself to sleep in her crib. That was it.

Or maybe it's just that she's the oldest child, and I've expected too much.

All of this self-blame was weighing on my heart like stones. By day I was processing, while by night I was waiting for a dream that never came. Finally, the cycle came to a halt when I got a call from my mother.

That may not seem unusual, but my mother had been dead for twenty years. The call didn't come in my dream—it came in my daughter's dream. One morning, she got up and said, "Mom, I had a dream that your mom called."

I perked up my ears. "Oh, who was it for?"

She said, "It was for you. She said she wanted to talk to you. I told her she couldn't because I know she's dead, but she insisted she wanted to talk to you. So, I told her I'd give you the message." And she did. My mother wanted to talk to me, and she came to me in my daughter's dream.

Suddenly I understood. In order for me to forgive myself for not being a perfect parent, I had to first forgive my own mother.

So, I went jogging. That may seem odd, but there's a place below the trail I jog on where three trees come together. When I want to be alone or to pray, I slide down off the path, and I put my hands on those trees. There I sense the presence of *Shekhinah*, the female manifestation of God, and I can feel the ancestors gathered to witness my prayers.

That day I slid down off the trail, sat down in the midst of the trees, and put my hands on the bark. I could feel the presence of Shekhinah. I felt the ancestors. And my mother was waiting.

In my mind, I heard her say, *It's time to forgive.*

I took a deep breath, and I tried.

"I forgive you for not being there when I needed you," I said, but the words seemed kind of hollow, wafting into the forest air.

I tried again. "I forgive you for drinking too much," I said, but I felt the words stick in my throat. I sensed my mother reaching out her arms and saying, *You can do it.*

I tried harder. "I forgive you," I said again, but the words just didn't seem real. I realized that those stones of unforgiveness that were wedged in my heart were actually warm and familiar. They had been there a long time. I thought, *What would I be without them?*

Instantly I heard my mother's voice say, *Lighter. You'd be lighter.*

I tried again. I tried harder. "I forgive you for drinking too much," I said, and this time I sensed the words rising up and floating into my mother's arms. I went on. "I forgive you for not being there when I needed you." Again, I felt her reach out and lift those words up, and I felt lighter.

With each word of forgiveness, I reached deeper inside. I could feel those stones shifting and rising, as I sensed my mother taking them, one by one, and I felt . . . lighter. When I was done, I leaned back and imagined I was floating in my mother's arms.

Eventually, I brushed myself off, climbed back up to the trail, and started to jog home. I felt so weightless that I was bounding down the trail. When I got home, I actually went to the bathroom and weighed myself. I weighed the same—physically, that is.

Now, the maggidah's daughter gently took the beggar's hand and spoke softly. "My mother's not waiting here for God's forgiveness. God has already forgiven her. My mother doesn't wait here because she needs your forgiveness. She waits here for your sake. She knows that malice stored up in the heart weighs like stones. She's waiting for you to let go of the malice. Come, it's time to forgive."

The beggar, who had suffered years of scorn and abuse, felt something shifting inside him. He walked slowly over to the maggidah, knelt, and took a deep breath. "I forgive you," he said. "Can you ever forgive me?"

The maggidah said, "Yes. It's done."

Then she slowly rose to her feet and helped the beggar up. She took off her prayer shawl and gently wrapped it around the beggar's shoulders. Then, together, they all walked to the next town.

ABOUT THE STORY

This story is a blend of a personal story with a story derived from the Talmud. The Talmudic story is adapted from Eric Kimmel's story, "Rabbi Eleazer and the Beggar" in his book, *Days of Awe: Stories for Rosh Hashanah and Yom Kippur.* The personal story is just as it happened, but with a few embellishments.

PART THREE

Freedom to Be Oneself

The Rooster Princess

LISA HUBERMAN

Once upon a time there was a queen whose daughter was her pride and joy. Her daughter was not only beautiful, but beloved by all for her ability to instantly make them feel at ease. If someone was sad, she knew just the right song or story to lift their spirits, and her remarkable memory helped her recall details from even the most inconsequential conversation. Whether courtier or peasant, she treated all with dignity and respect, and everyone agreed that she would grow into a graceful and noble queen.

One morning, however, all of that changed. As the palace awoke, there was a loud crowing sound coming from the princess's chamber. Afraid that one of the roosters had broken free, they sent one of the royal farmers to wrangle it, but to everyone's shock, the sound was coming from the princess. She was perched in her petticoats on the railing of the windowsill, her arms folded like wings, with pillow feathers strewn through her wild hair. When anyone tried to approach her, she let out a loud "bawk!" and chased them out of the room.

When the queen demanded to know why her daughter was absent from breakfast, the servants shifted nervously, until one of them blurted out, "The princess has been possessed!"

The queen rushed to her daughter's chamber. She was horrified by what she saw. She summoned all of the kingdom's best experts—doctors, sorcerers, alchemists—but none could cure the princess's ailment.

The royal servants, out of loyalty to the queen, kept the princess's true condition a secret and told anyone who asked that she had fallen gravely ill. With the potential loss of the heir, the queen wondered how long it would be before other kingdoms began clamoring to take over.

One night the palace received a mysterious visitor: a woman in a dark cloak, whose face was ageless.

"I am here to help the princess," she said to a servant, who then brought the mysterious visitor to the queen.

"What could you possibly do that the greatest sorcerers and physicians could not?" the queen asked.

"Give me a week," the visitor said. "You might as well let me try."

The servant began showing the woman to her guest quarters, but the woman asked to see the princess first.

When the servant knocked on the door of the princess's room, the mysterious visitor stayed the servant's hand. "I'll see myself in," she said.

"Are you sure?" asked the servant. "The princess can be … a lot to handle."

"I'll let you know if I need anything."

After the servant departed, the woman cracked the door open and observed the princess for a few moments. The princess strutted and squawked about the room, bobbing her head as she walked, shaking the feathers she had stuck to her arms.

The visitor silently entered. Then she stripped off her garments, down to the petticoats and bloomers, and began to move around the room in much the same manner as the princess.

The princess stopped strutting and eyed this new intruder suspiciously. Then she crouched, ready to attack.

The intruder started pecking at the princess's bowl of corn.

The rooster princess went berserk. She lunged and squealed in the intruder's face. "Squawk! Who are you?! Squawk!"

But the woman remained calm and said, "A rooster. Just like you."

"No, you're not!" the princess squawked.

"If you're a rooster, why can't I be? Did you really think you were the only rooster in the kingdom?"

The princess thought about this for a moment. "What do you want?"

"The winds were getting cold outside, and I heard you had a warm barn. I thought I might take shelter. If you'll have me?"

The princess circled the intruder a few times, inspecting her. "Fine. But stay away from my grain!"

All night, the servant in the adjoining chamber slept with one eye open, ready for the sound of the mysterious visitor screaming from the princess's chamber. But to her surprise, when she entered the chamber in the morning, she found not one but two roosters, squawking and strutting about.

The roosters continued for three days in this manner, until one day the princess asked the visiting woman, "How did you know you were a rooster?"

The woman thought for a minute and replied, "I didn't always. But when I saw you being such a happy rooster, I suppose it awakened something in me that I hadn't thought about before. Do you know what I mean?"

"Yes," the princess crowed. "I was out one day making a royal visit to one of our subjects' farms—the same sort of thing as usual—they presented their vegetables, their cheese, their animals, and they bowed, and I curtsied. I had done the same thing at three other farms that day and, though I was nodding and curtsying and smiling like I was supposed to, it was all soooo boring. But then when the farmer went to get his chickens, the rooster flew out and landed right on top of me. The farmer kept apologizing and bowing, begging not to be sent to the dungeon, but it was the most exciting thing that had happened to me all day.

"When I got back to the palace and had to sit through another boring royal dinner, I kept thinking about that rooster. How he just seemed so free—he didn't have to care if his posture was correct, which spoon he used for which course, or the name of some stupid prince who wanted to propose marriage. So, the next morning, as the sun was coming up, I got on the edge of my bed and crowed. And it felt right!"

"And now you're happy."

The princess hesitated. "Can I tell you a secret? Sometimes I get sick of eating corn."

"Then why don't you ask for something else?"

"Because I'm a rooster, and roosters eat corn."

"You can be a rooster who eats whatever you like."

The princess considered this. "And what if ... sometimes I miss going to balls?"

"You can be a rooster who goes to balls."

"Yes, but if I went to a ball, people would be upset if I was a rooster, and I don't want to go back to having to be a princess again."

The woman thought for a second. "If you can be a rooster who goes to balls, why can't you be a princess who sometimes acts like a rooster?"

"When I act like a rooster, it makes my mother unhappy."

"But acting like a princess makes *you* unhappy. Don't you think she should know that?"

When a week had passed, the princess and the woman emerged from the chamber. To everyone's amazement, the princess seemed restored to her former, graceful self.

"I honestly did not believe you could do it," the queen said.

The woman bowed. "I am glad to be of service."

The queen beckoned to her daughter, "Now that this nonsense is over, we must host a ball to present you to the kingdom—so everyone will know things will go back to normal."

For a moment, the princess looked like she was about to comply. But then she paused, opened her mouth and let out a "SQUAWK!"

"I thought you had fixed her!"

"Mother, it is true that she helped me to behave once again as a princess. But make no mistake, I will always be a rooster. And if you cannot accept me as I am, then I will return to my room, and you can find another plan for the kingdom."

And so, the rooster princess grew to be the rooster queen, who was known throughout the land as being a wise and unconventional ruler, who always allowed everyone in her court—human or fowl—to express who they were.

ABOUT THE STORY

I first encountered this story as "The Rooster Who Would Be King" in *Jewish Stories One Generation Tells Another* by Peninnah Schram. The story itself originates with Rebbe Nachman of Breslov and has been told many times over. As a queer person who also wrestles with neurodivergence, I resonated with the portrayal of someone who suddenly decides to stop fitting into the role designed for them, and how their life is changed by the arrival of a powerful teacher who understands them. I changed the prince to a princess here to further align with my own desire to rebel against the gender box assigned to me at birth.

The Day Elijah Saved My Life

BATYA PODOS

Nice Jewish girls don't go into the theatre. They marry nice Jewish boys and have nice Jewish children and, preferably, live within walking distance, or a short car ride, from their mothers. But I wanted to be an actress, which to my parents meant I was a breath away from being a streetwalker.

"What about Barbra Streisand?" I'd throw at my parents. "What about Lauren Bacall? What about Goldie Hawn?" Really? That cute little blond is Jewish?

My parents' disapproval of my theatrical aspirations was loud. They lost no opportunity to tell me how I would ruin my life if I pursued my dream. But it was my mother who took me to see my first play, *The Music Man*, on Broadway, so it was her fault I fell in love with the theatre when I was ten. Much to my parents' disappointment, I got my B.A. in drama, then went on to study at Goodman Theatre in Chicago. I was hopeless. I was smitten. I quoted lines from plays I had studied or acted in; I went around singing songs from musicals. It was my passion, my calling.

And it was hard—working, studying, auditioning and rehearsing, never having money or certainty about what might come next. With no one to urge me on but my own desire, it became unsustainable. Somewhere between auditions, artistic poverty (which is only romantic in movies), and the lack of parental support, things began to unravel.

One day in the middle of a performance, I lost my nerve. I barely made it to curtain call.

Auditions became painful; going to the theatre made me burst into tears. I turned away from my heart's desire to save myself. I moved to Santa Monica, not too far from my parents. I went to work for an insurance company. I had no purpose, no joy. I went through the motions of living.

I moved into a tiny apartment three blocks from the Santa Monica beach, looking over the remains of Pacific Ocean Park—a failed amusement park that was slowly crumbling to ruins in the sea air. At every opportunity, I'd walk to the beach and peer through the chain link fence that housed rides and concessions and strangely built creatures designed to delight, but no longer able to fulfill their purpose.

Almost daily, I would stand at the very edge of the waves and look out over the Pacific towards the horizon. I was twenty-something, filled with my own disappointment and loss, and it became the drama of my life. One day, I wondered what would happen if I walked into the sea. Understand this: I was not suicidal. The actual thought of dying never occurred to me. It was the romance of it. I wanted to be swept away in a theatrical moment. I wanted to be free.

I took off my sandals and, fully dressed, walked into the waves. Like Nachshon, who, legend tells us, was the first to walk into the water of the Red Sea before it split, I walked up to my knees, my thighs, my waist—my eyes never leaving that horizon, the curve of the earth that was calling me. I had an image of floating forever, carried off by the water without a care in the world, overwhelmed by the beauty of it all.

It was then, I heard a voice. I turned to see a dark-skinned man with large brown eyes standing, fully dressed, next to me in the water. I don't know how he managed to come up next to me without me seeing him. "I have always loved the ocean," he was saying, with the lilt of India in his voice. "You must love it too. Why don't we go get a coffee?"

My bubble was shattered. I stared at him with disbelief, buffeted by the waves. We were further out than I had realized. He went on. "Maybe we could get a meal or take in a movie." I couldn't believe it. I was trying to have a poetic experience, and he wanted a date. My precious, transcendent moment was ruined. I refused to acknowledge him. Angrily, I turned my back on the ocean and struggled to shore. But he was still at my side, still talking. I grabbed my sandals and, dripping, made my way home. I never saw him again.

Almost instantly, everything in my life changed. I moved to San Francisco. I became a feminist, went back to school for my master's, and began writing and producing plays. I eventually moved to the UK where I began my journey as a storyteller. I discovered teaching was a passion that surpassed the stage. My world cracked open like a pinata, and I was grabbing the candy. And I totally forgot about the incident at the beach.

Thirty years later, it was my privilege to study to become a *maggid*—storyteller and teacher in the Jewish tradition. I had, over the years, become a professional storyteller, telling stories and teaching throughout Europe and the U.S. I told stories from all over the world, but until I began training as a maggid, I had never told a Jewish story. I was willing and I was learning, but when my teacher told us we had to tell a true story, I panicked.

In over twenty years of storytelling, I had never told a true story, shared my real-life experiences with an audience. But Devorah insisted this was a skill I needed to learn. "I don't have any stories," I complained. Inside, I whined "Don't make me do this!" I didn't confess that personal stories made me feel exposed and vulnerable and that once my maggid training was over, I'd never tell one again.

I meditated on my life, going back into childhood, and still could find nothing worthy of telling. Then suddenly, like a door blown open by the wind, I remembered walking into the water of the Pacific. My memory returned in such vivid detail that it shocked me. It had been buried all these years and had ceased to exist until that spark of revelation. I suddenly understood that the stranger with the Indian lilt to his voice had saved my life that day. Although my intention was never to end it, had I gone much further into the water, I would have been swept away, and it would have been nothing like my romantic fantasy.

How could I have forgotten something so important? They say there's an angel who touches the newborn's lips so they will forget the secrets they were born with. I'm quite certain that my memory of that event had been taken from me until I was ready to understand it and use it. And what I understood was that I had been visited by the prophet Elijah in the guise of my Indian savior—Elijah, a shapeshifter, who disguises himself so he can weigh the human heart and reward those who prove worthy.

I'm not sure how worthy my heart was that day on the beach, but I do know that I was given a chance to allow it to grow and mature.

Nice Jewish girls do become actors, but this is one girl who didn't. I still love the theatre and go whenever I can. I still cry watching the Tony Awards on television. But my work as a storyteller and teacher has been richer and deeper than any I could imagine having, had I followed my first love. My parents would be proud. Now, if only I had married that nice Jewish boy ...

ABOUT THE STORY

It's difficult to write about a true encounter with divine intervention. Many of us have been visited by angels or other supernatural beings at difficult times in our lives with life-changing results. Most often, it is the stranger who shows up at the exact moment you need them. Yet, there is always the fear, when telling one of these stories, that you will appear too imaginative for your own good.

All I know is, it really happened. I didn't make it up. And whenever I tell this story, someone comes up to me and shares a similar experience. So, my wish is that you remain open to the unexplained, and should Elijah show up at your side, welcome him in.

Holding Her Own

DEBRA GORDON ZASLOW

LONG AGO, Rabbi Yeshaya of Poland had a wife, Havva, who gave him constant trouble. She was always praying, morning to night, all day long. She would walk around with her nose in a prayer book, murmuring to herself, not paying attention to anybody else.

After Reb Yeshaya returned home from the synagogue after morning prayers, he would ask, "What's for breakfast, Havveleh?" only to hear, "Shhh! I'm praying! Don't interrupt!"

It was no better for him at lunchtime. He would say, as politely as could be, "Dearest, what is for lunch?" to which she'd answer, "Can't you see I'm busy? I'm in the middle of saying Psalms."

At dinnertime, when he approached her with, "Havveleh, what have you made for dinner?" She answered, "I can't make food. I'm not done reciting the holy texts. Please stop disturbing me!"

Later, if he asked for a cup of tea, she said, "You want a cup of tea? You'll have to make it yourself. I can't be concerned with physical matters."

So, naturally, Reb Yeshaya was quite unhappy at home. One day he came to Havva with a book in his hand, pointing to a page. "The sages say right here, 'What is a good wife? Someone who does her husband's bidding.'"

She answered him without hesitation. "Really? Well, the sages also say, 'Whoever is occupied with doing a *mitzvah* (commandment) is excused from the obligation to perform a different mitzvah.' And I'm constantly doing a mitzvah—the mitzvah of praying. So, let me be!"

The next day, Reb Yeshaya came back with another book. "Look at this," he said. "The Torah, in the book of Exodus, says that the pious Jewish women were involved in the building of the Tabernacle in the Sinai. The verse refers to '*All the women* whose hearts were stirred with wisdom.'"

Havva stared at him blankly. "So?"

He continued, gesturing at the page, "So, here, in another section of Esther, it says, '*All the women* should honor their husbands.' So, the use of this repeated phrase shows that even pious women doing the mitzvah of building the temple were not excused from obeying their husbands' will and doing their bidding all the time."

Havva glared at him. "Really? Seriously? You're quoting me from the book of Esther? Do you think I don't know the scriptures? That's the part where King Ahasuerus's friends convince him to kill his wife, Queen Vashti, because she won't obey him and dance naked for them! Is that what you want?" She screamed at him, "Do you want to kill me because I won't do your bidding?"

Reb Yeshaya hollered back, "No! No, I … I don't want that! I don't want to kill you."

"Then what is it that you want?"

He paused and took a breath. "Well, I just … I just want … what I want is to eat, actually. I'm hungry."

Havva stared back at him, and then she paused. She nodded slowly. "Me too," she said. "I'm really hungry."

Reb Yeshaya asked, "Do you think you could show me how to cook an egg?"

She agreed, and they went into the kitchen. While she taught him to cook eggs, they talked about some points of Torah. Then they slowly ate breakfast together.

From then on, they prayed and studied Torah together every day. They discussed each verse, naturally arguing vigorously over every interpretation. And, of course, they began to cook alongside each other each day and enjoyed their hearty meals together. I'm told neither one of them ever went hungry again.

ABOUT THE STORY

I encountered this story, called "Standing up for Herself," in Yitzhak Buxbaum's *Jewish Tales of Holy Women*. It ends with the husband admonishing his wife with words of Torah to show her that "pious women … are not exempt from … serving their husbands and doing their will at every hour and time."

After his version Buxbaum notes, "The tale is told from the man's side and does not record Rebbitzen Havva's response to her husband's final comment. It seems unlikely that she agreed with him; if she had, her submission would have been noted. Perhaps her retort was censored, or she let him have the last word." In my version, I decided it was time to let her have the last word.

This adaptation is offered with the permission of the Estate of Yitzhak Buxbaum.

The Fishmonger and the Shiviti

AYALA SARAH ZONNENSCHEIN

I N AUGUST 1895, there was a severe drought in the little village of Chigavoy Gebernya. This village, not far from the Black Sea in what was then Russia, is where my grandmother, of blessed memory, was born. When I was a little girl, she made me say the name over and over so that I would remember it.

The people in Chigavoy Gebernya were literally dying from thirst. The wise man of the village decreed communal fasts on Tuesdays and Thursdays, as was customary in times of peril, and the people prayed, but their prayers were not answered. The villagers were so distraught that they pleaded with *Hashem*, "Please, Holy One, have mercy on us. Give us water!"

Finally, the Holy One heard their cries and appeared to the *hacham*, the wise man, in a dream, saying, "Do not continue to pray, because your prayers will not be answered—not until the one person in your village who is the most worthy to lead the prayers on behalf of your people, will come to pray with you."

The hacham asked, "Who should we get to pray with us? Who is the most worthy?"

The Holy One answered, "Shayndl the Fishmonger!"

At this, the hacham woke suddenly from his sleep, wondering, *How can this be, that the Holy Blessed One wants Shayndl to pray for us?*

She's a very simple woman, completely ignorant of the Torah. How can her prayers help? Certainly, my dream was nonsense!

He went back to sleep, but as soon as he drifted off, he dreamed again. This time the Holy One said, "Don't bother to pray and plead. If that fishmonger does not lead the prayers, your prayers will not be answered!"

The hacham awoke again with a start, but this time his wife, Zelda, woke up as well. He said to her, "Zelda, how can it be? Hashem came to me in my dreams, twice, and told me that Shayndl the Fishmonger is the only one in all Chigavoy Gebernya who is worthy enough to lead our prayers. Everyone knows she is not just a simple woman but probably the simplest woman among us."

Zelda replied, "If you dreamt this once, you might say this is nonsense, but since Hashem came to you in your dreams twice, I think you had better pay attention."

The following morning, the hacham told the townspeople to gather tomorrow at the synagogue to pray again for rain. "Who will lead the prayers?" the people asked.

"Tomorrow, we'll see who is worthy to lead our prayers," the wise man answered. He was ashamed to say that the fishmonger would, because they all knew she was a simple woman who did not know Torah at all!

The next day, when everyone came to the *shul*, they asked the hacham who he'd chosen to lead the prayers. The hacham looked around but didn't see the fishmonger. He wasn't surprised, really, since Shayndl never came to shul.

So, embarrassed to say what Hashem had told him in the dream, he told the villagers, "If Hashem is to answer our prayers, we need to gather every single soul who lives in Chigavoy Gebernya in the shul to pray for rain. Then we shall see who is most worthy, but we won't know who that is until all are here together."

"Who is missing in our holy gathering this morning?" the wise man asked everyone.

The villagers looked around, accounting for all their town's folk, they thought, until someone noticed that Shayndl the Fishmonger was not among them.

"Go fetch Shayndl and tell her we need her to pray with us for the rains!"

A few of the womenfolk went down to Shayndl's shop and asked her to come to help pray for rain. Reluctantly, she removed her apron, washed her hands—which always smelled of fish—and followed them to the shul.

When they arrived, the hacham immediately called the fishmonger to him and told her to go before the ark to lead the prayers. "Are you making fun of me because I'm just a simple woman?" asked Shayndl. "I don't know any of the prayers and can barely pronounce the *Shema!*"

"What will be, will be," replied the hacham. "Just pray from your heart."

The fishmonger tried to pray. She closed her eyes and earnestly searched for the words, but no prayer would come. She worried what the villagers would think of her, and suddenly she ran out of the shul.

The villagers, wringing their hands in worry, cried out to the hacham, "What should we do? Find someone else to lead the prayers?"

"Not so fast," said the hacham. "Let's just wait a little and see."

No one understood what they were waiting for. A few minutes passed, and then suddenly the fishmonger returned carrying the scale from her shop and went straight to the *bimah*, the platform, at the front of the shul. Everyone watched in amazement. Some snickering was heard, and laughter rose up from the crowd.

"What is she going to do now, weigh out her fish in the shul?"

The fishmonger stood quietly looking at them until a hush fell over the crowd. She spoke softly, saying, "I am a simple woman. I don't even know the prayers. But *Shiviti Hashem L'negdi Tamid*—I have Hashem before me always." She pointed to her scale.

"Here is the *yud*," She pointed to the two pans of the balance and continued, "And here is the *hey*." Then pointing to the vertical bar, she said, "And this is a *vav*." Then she showed the base of the scale and said, "And here is the final *hey* that spells out the Holy One's name. All day when I am weighing out my fish for customers, I see the Holy One before me."

The fishmonger looked up to heaven and said, "*Ribbono shel Olam*, Master of the Universe, if I have ever cheated even once with my weights and blemished the letters of Your great and holy name, YHVH, let fire come down from heaven and burn me to ashes immediately! But if I have never cheated or stolen from anyone and never blemished your holy name, then I beg You, Master of All the Worlds, to turn to us with mercy and send us abundant rain!"

As soon as she finished speaking, the skies quickly darkened. Gray clouds gathered, and blessed rain poured down in torrents from heaven. The people were amazed and cheered, "Heaven bless Shayndl the Fishmonger, whose prayers were answered on our behalf!"

Suddenly the hacham stood up and, when all was quiet, said to them, "Hashem came to me in a dream telling me our prayers would not be answered until Shayndl the Fishmonger prayed on our behalf. I was afraid to tell you for fear you would laugh and ridicule me. But now you've seen that though we have great sages among us, none of our prayers were answered until Shayndl prayed for us, and then our prayers were answered immediately, in the merit of our holy fishmonger."

You see, it's not so important what we know and how much we've learned, or even if we are a man or a woman. What is important is to show up and open our hearts when we pray to God. *Shiviti Hashem L'negdi Tamid,* place God before me always. If we, like the fishmonger, can place Hashem before us always, our hearts will open, our entire beings will come into balance, and the Holy One will hear our prayers.

ABOUT THE STORY

I first heard a version of this story in 2000 from Maggid Jhos Singer. Jhos told me he heard it from the Samborer Rebbe, Rabbi Herschel Yolles, of blessed memory. The Rebbe did not name his source. The closest version in print is "A Question of Balance" in *Jewish Stories One Generation Tells Another* by Peninnah Schram. I liked the Jhos Singer version, via the Samborer Rebbe version, which describes the scales as a *shiviti*, containing the letters of the unpronounceable holy name of God, YHVH. I changed the male fishmonger in Jhos's telling to a female fishmonger.

The Shekhinah Is in Exile

DEBRA GORDON ZASLOW

ONCE THERE was a man and a woman who prayed for many years to have a child. Eventually they were blessed with a baby, but it wasn't exactly what they wanted. They were hoping for a boy, but this was a girl. And as their little girl grew, it became apparent she was a unique and wild child.

She would race around, stomping her feet, making noise, and getting dirty. She would run off into the woods where she climbed trees and rescued stray animals. They called her a *vilda chaya*, a wild thing. She wanted to be outside all the time, talking with the trees and animals, but hardly ever talking to people. Instead of speaking, she had a little wooden flute that she played whenever she was excited or passionate about something. Even though the music was quite delightful, she played it in all the wrong places.

Her parents didn't know what to do with her. At school she would jump up from her desk and race into the woods if a butterfly flew by the window. When it was time to sit quietly to study or read, she'd pull out her flute and play music. Of course, they couldn't bring her to synagogue because when she got excited by the prayers and songs, she'd play her flute and disturb everyone, so they kept her away.

One year on Yom Kippur, her parents decided it was time to try again. She was getting older, and they wanted her to practice being more civilized. Thinking it would be good for her to sit and listen to prayers, they brought her to the synagogue with strict instructions to stay in her seat and pay attention to the services.

She did try, for a while. But when she heard the voices rising in song and prayer, she couldn't contain herself, and she reached for her flute. Her father put his hand on hers and whispered, "No!"

When the prayers got more intense, she grew more excited and reached for her flute again. This time her father pulled the flute away from her.

Toward the end of the service, as the praying began to ascend to the gates of heaven, the girl got so excited, she reached over and grabbed the flute back from her father. This time he grabbed her, pulled her out of her seat, and led her out of the synagogue. He walked with her into a clearing nearby. "Wait here," he said. You can play your flute. Just stay here!"

When he came back into the synagogue, he saw things weren't going as expected. The rabbi had stopped the service and was pacing back and forth, muttering to himself. The people were upset since they had been praying and fasting all day, so they were tired and hungry. One of the congregants went up to the rabbi and asked, "Is something wrong? Why aren't we finishing the prayers?"

The rabbi kept pacing and answered. "I ... I ... don't know ... something is missing. I can't go on. Something is missing."

"What's missing? "

The rabbi stood still. "I'll have to answer you with a story," he said.

"Once there was a king and queen whose daughter was getting married. This was cause for great celebration in the community. Everyone in the kingdom was invited to a lavish wedding that promised a great feast with all the trimmings. Unfortunately, a few days before the wedding, the princess took ill and died. All the people were in mourning. That is, all except one man, who showed up on the day of the wedding, banging on the palace gates, demanding the five-course dinner that was promised to him on the invitation."

Now the rabbi turned to the congregation and asked, "Do you

want me to be like that boorish man, banging at the gates, demanding to be admitted to the celebration, even though the princess is dead? Should I stand at the gates of heaven and demand entry? How can I? How can I, when the *Shekhinah* is in exile?"

Nobody in the congregation had any idea what the rabbi was talking about, except the girl's father. He got up and walked out of the synagogue until he found his daughter in the clearing. She was crouched under a tree playing her flute, softly. He beckoned to her, took her by the hand, and led her back into the synagogue.

When she walked in, everyone in the congregation turned. She slowly brought the flute to her lips and began to play.

The music flowed out sweet and melodious, pouring forth with tears of the deepest sorrow and laughter of the angels. The melody filled the room with the whispers of the ancestors, and the voices of the women, *kolay ha nashim*. The notes soared into the hearts of everyone in the synagogue with the fullness of melancholy and the sweet softness of clouds. As the music rose higher and higher with each note, it lifted all of the prayers in all of the hearts…. straight up through the gates of heaven.

ABOUT THE STORY

Each week on Shabbat, we welcome the Shekhinah, the female presence of God, she who dwells within. We have to invite her, because the sense of her presence can come and go. One year, on *Shabbat Shuva*, the Shabbat of Return, between Rosh Hashanah and Yom Kippur, I was inspired to create this story. It's a variation on a famous Baal Shem Tov story about a mute boy with a flute. In my version a young girl, who loves nature, uplifts the congregation with her flute.

A Queer Soul in the Shtetl

LISA HUBERMAN

IN A tiny *shtetl* in Ukraine there was a girl named Beyle who sold herring from her cart. As she grew it became clear that Beyle was not the sort of girl that anyone had in mind. Beyle had a low masculine voice, a mess of unruly red hair, and walked about with hard and heavy steps.

"She's not a regular girl, but she's not a boy either," the townspeople would say.

Beyle pretended not to hear the townspeople's chatter—she dove into the work of hauling the herring and pushing her cart, day after day, and tried not to think about how much of a disappointment she was to her father.

Years earlier, when Beyle was still a child, she was once caught roughhousing with the boys. While Beyle's father was unconcerned, the townspeople made their disapproval clear and said, "The evil eye is upon her! You must find a cure!"

So Beyle's father took his daughter on the half-day journey to the yeshiva three villages over, to consult with Talmudic experts. He managed to gain an audience with the *rosh yeshiva*, the head rabbi.

Her father pleaded, "Rebbe, I love my daughter, and I fear it is perhaps my fault for the way she has turned out. Her mother died young, and I raised her as a boy, the only way I knew how—please, will you fix her?"

But the rabbi only scratched his beard and said, "God will provide."

Time passed, and eventually Beyle stopped roughhousing with the boys—mainly because they excluded her as they began to pursue brides. But while other girls in the shtetl developed shapely figures as they moved into womanhood, Beyle simply got taller, towering over any potential suitors. Eventually the local matchmaker managed to find a husband for Beyle, but the groom's family broke it off when they discovered Beyle had a habit of sneaking into the men's side of the sanctuary during Shabbat prayers.

Again, Beyle's father went to visit the rabbi. And again, the the rabbi scratched his beard and said, "God will provide."

By this time, Beyle's father had given up on any clear remedy, and he became comforted by the fact his daughter would forever work with him in the fish market. They settled into a silent routine of preparing herring for sale—sorting, descaling, skinning in an almost dance-like fashion.

There was one person to whom Beyle could unburden herself. This was her friend Rachel, the daughter of the owner of the tavern to which she made deliveries every Friday before Shabbat. Rachel was the complete opposite of Beyle in every way—smooth-complexioned, shapely, with chestnut hair and a porcelain doll face. In a songbird voice, Rachel would fill Beyle in on all of the local gossip, making Beyle feel like she was part of the social fabric of the shtetl. Unlike Beyle, Rachel was not wanting for admirers, and often Beyle would see a crowd of potential suitors waiting outside the door.

Beyle said to her one day, "I don't know why you would bother spending so much time with me—surely one of these men would be much better company."

Rachel gazed in the direction of her potential suitors and scoffed, "Oh yes, how thrilling to have the same conversation over and over about how many children they want and the number of goats in my dowry. Besides, you are more of a gentleman than those dolts could ever be."

Beyle persisted, "But wouldn't a good marriage please your father? My father would be so happy if I had so many prospects."

Rachel looked into Beyle's eyes, took her hand and said, "But what would make *you* happy?"

Beyle was speechless. No one had ever thought to ask her such a question. Something electric had started to course through her at Rachel's touch. As if compelled by some force of magic, Beyle found her mouth drawn ever so close to Rachel's, consumed by an insatiable hunger …

Unfortunately, it was at this very moment that Rachel's mother chose to enter and screamed, "Oy vey! What is the meaning of this?" Rachel's parents went straight to Beyle's father and yelled, "Beyle is not content to ruin her own life—but also the life of our Rachel as well! Something must be done!"

Beyle hung her head and said, "I'm so sorry father. I wish I knew how to be better, but I do not know how to fix myself."

So Beyle and her father traveled to consult with the rabbi. But this time, it was Beyle who spoke.

She said, "Please, Rebbe, my father is poor and growing old. I know I am not the sort of daughter who can make him proud by marrying well. You said before, 'God will provide,' but I am asking you. Right here. Right now."

The Rebbe stroked his beard and looked like he was about to recite a prayer or consult scripture, but instead he wrote something down on a piece of parchment and handed it to Beyle. It read—"The problem that you face is beyond my own scope. But perhaps this Professor in Odessa will be able to help you in ways I cannot."

So for the first time, Beyle prepared to leave her shtetl. "Don't worry Papa, you'll see. I'll come back, and all our problems will be solved."

Beyle traveled many miles, over hills and valleys, to reach Odessa. When she got off the train, her eyes widened as she stared at sites grander than anything she could have imagined. Aromas of strange foods combined with fine perfumes greeted her, as well the stench of rats and human waste.

Everything moved so fast, and the people walked so swiftly that she feared she might get trampled. She wanted to flee, but she was also fascinated by the people around her: men laughing as they marched down the street, arms locked and laughing with wild abandon as if they were lovers. Beyle was so entranced by a woman in a grand floral skirt with a bird on her shoulder, that she crashed right into her.

Beyle stammered, "Forgive me, madam, I was not looking—"

It was the bird who answered, "Squack! Watch where you're going, *podonok!*"

Beyle was struck speechless. The woman beckoned the creature to her and stroked its neck. To Beyle's surprise, the woman spoke with what sounded like the deep voice of a man. "Now where are you wandering, little goat? You seemed to have strayed far from your pasture."

Still unable to form words, Beyle dug out the crumpled paper with the professor's address and handed it over.

"Ah, you are one of the professor's flock. Come. I shall shepherd you there and shield you from the wolves!"

Beyle followed until they came to the address, and a man answered the door. He wore a sleek, pin-striped suit with a violet vest and a gold pocket chain.

The man asked, "And who might you be?"

Beyle sputtered, "I-Krovozner–train–cure–"

"You are the one the Rebbe sent?"

Beyle nodded.

"Are you planning to spend the day in the doorway, or would you like to come in?"

She stepped into the house and jumped as the door closed behind her.

The professor examined her, "I suppose you have a name, then?"

Beyle mumbled under her breath. "Beyle."

The professor shook his head. "That's not your name."

"I'm not sure what you—"

"That may have been the name your parents gave you—they may have thought when you were born that you were a young girl named Beyle. But that does not mean that's actually who you are."

"I—how did you—"

"Because my father, the Rebbe, made the same error at my birth. Now young man, tell me: what is your name?"

The young man, who truly felt seen for the first time, stared at the professor in stunned silence. After a moment, he took a deep breath, cleared his throat, threw back his shoulders, and said in a booming voice, "Berel. My name is Berel."

"Very good. Let's get you a proper suit, then."

The professor snapped his fingers and had a servant send for the local tailor.

The tailor motioned for Berel to remove his dress. He felt like a snake shedding his skin. When he tried the suit coat on, he felt like a new person.

Over the next few weeks, Berel accompanied the Professor on his social engagements. When Berel and the Professor walked down the street, Berel was self-conscious that people were staring—but it was not out of ridicule. For the first time in his life, Berel had admirers who were delighted and fascinated by this new exotic arrival from the country.

But Berel missed his home. He missed his father. He missed Rachel and wished she were there to see this—the museums, the literary talks, the parks, the new foods and music. Even though the city was exciting, he missed the stillness of the shtetl. He missed the smell of herring.

When he made his plans known to the professor, he did not protest, and he furnished him with provisions and funds for the journey.

Berel said, "I don't know how I could repay you."

His eyes welled up, and he embraced the young man, saying, "May he who rewarded you with all goodness, reward you with all goodness forever. My door will always be open."

As Berel gazed out the train window on the ride home, the tall buildings and bustle of the city gave way to the calm of the countryside. And as the train pulled into the station at Krovozer, a crowd of villagers assembled. It was rare that anyone should leave Krovozer—it was even more unusual for anyone who left to return.

The assembled crowd, expecting a young woman, was shocked

to find a tall, dashing, redheaded young man in his place. The crowd parted, and Berel gulped as he caught his father's eye. Berel extended a nervous hand, "Papa?"

Berel's heart pounded as his father surveyed him. After what felt like an eternity, his father embraced him. His father said, "My child, it is good to have you home."

And it was good to be home. After the noise and chaos of Odessa, Berel was comforted to return to the simple routine of the shtetl. He was glad to see the predictable dirt road to the market where he could take in the natural beauty of the seasons, and to see a sky not clouded with buildings and city smoke. The smell of fresh herring in his nostrils and even the aches in his muscles as he pulled the cart made him feel alive.

Berel was surprised at how easily the men of the village accepted him into their fold. Perhaps there was something about how naturally he fit his current form. While Beyle had slumped in ill-fitting women's dress, Berel now radiated confidence. Beyle's unruly mop of red hair caught the light dramatically when shaped onto Berel's head. The men of the village welcomed him in to pray and showed him how to properly wrap tefillin. And even when one old man made a snide remark about a girl being in the men's section of the shul, he was quickly silenced.

Everyone in Krovozer seemed captivated by the newly returned arrival from the city—except the one whose attention Berel desired the most.

During shul, while all of the women admiringly leaned over the balcony in an attempt to meet Berel's gaze, Rachel remained consumed in prayer. When Berel stopped to make a delivery at the tavern, it was one of Rachel's younger sisters who received him. Berel inquired as to Rachel's whereabouts, and her sister said she was at the dressmaker's.

Berel rushed to the dressmaker's and saw Rachel exiting the shop with her mother. Their eyes met and time stopped. Rachel turned to her mother, "You go on ahead and put the dress in the trunk. I'll join you in a moment."

Berel made an awkward bow and said, "Good day."

Rachel replied, "I'm surprised such a man of the world notices someone as plain as myself."

Berel asked, "Have I done something to offend you?"

Rachel said, "You disappeared for months. Vanished into thin air. No letter. I had to hear about your adventures through village gossip."

Berel got down on one knee and pleaded, "I wanted to write, but what was happening to me—I didn't know how to start. But if you'll allow me, I'd like to spend the rest of my life trying."

Rachel never did marry the butcher's son. The village elders had certain *halachic* questions about the legality of a union between Rachel and Berel, given the Jewish commandment to continue one's family line, so they appealed to the judgment of the rabbi. After several weeks, the rabbi returned his ruling. He cited the example of Sarah from the Torah, whose lack of a womb did not prevent God from blessing her as the mother of the Jewish nation.

Berel and Rachel were married after *Shavuot*, in a celebration that would be part of the village lore for centuries to come. The rabbi himself presided over the ceremony, and the procession was accompanied by a band from Odessa. At the wedding feast, Berel's father stood to give his toast, but instead beckoned to the professor in the back of the hall.

After a moment, the professor rose and lifted his glass to Berel and Rachel, "To the young couple—May your love blaze a path that remakes the world for us all."

ABOUT THE STORY

I first encountered the story of Berel-Beyle through a podcast interview with Noam Sienna about his anthology, *A Rainbow Thread*. The story originates in a 1937 letter to the editor in the Yiddish *Forward*. The idea of a gender-transition story set in the Ukrainian shtetl—let alone an uplifting one—completely captivated me. The story came to be even more resonant for me as I made my way through a personal gender journey during the pandemic, adapting a more masculine presentation. What was missing from the original story, however, was Berel-Beyle's own voice and inner life, which I have attempted to uplift here.

PART FOUR
Gifts We Give and Recieve

Esperanza and the Twelve Loaves of Challah

GAIL PASTERNACK

LONG AGO, a woman by the name of Esperanza lived with her husband in Barcelona, Spain. Esperanza was an expert baker, as were her mother and her grandmother before her. She ran a small bakery that drew customers from all over Barcelona. And while Esperanza was proud of that, she was still sad.

Esperanza's and her husband's families were *conversos,* Jews who had been forced to convert to Christianity after Queen Isabella and King Ferdinand rose to power and united Spain as a Catholic country. Secretly, at home, behind closed curtains, Esperanza lit *Shabbat* candles every Friday evening. She would say the *Shema* quietly so no one would hear and report them to the authorities. Sadly, those were the only Jewish traditions she knew, for her parents had been too afraid of the Inquisition courts to teach her anything else.

She craved to live more fully as a Jew. Her husband craved that too, so one night, they packed up everything they could carry and left Barcelona. A merchant friend of theirs got them passage on a ship to Genoa. From there they managed to get to Athens, and then finally, after months of travel, they arrived in Jerusalem.

Everything they saw amazed them. Men wore *yarmulkes* publicly, out on the street. Shops were closed for Shabbat. And the market sold kosher food!

Esperanza wanted to jump for joy, but then she realized how little she knew about her own faith. She didn't know Hebrew. Other than the Shema, she didn't know any of the prayers. And while she knew how to bake bread, she didn't know how to make the challah that all her new neighbors baked for the Sabbath.

Esperanza and her husband settled in as best they could. He found work, and she made friends. She became especially close to Shayna, the woman who lived next door to her. Shayna taught Esperanza how to bake challah, and soon Esperanza became known for her challah, which had the most delightful sweetness and the perfect chewy texture. Even more important, she began to attend synagogue every Sabbath.

One Saturday, Esperanza and Shayna sat in their seats upstairs at the synagogue as the rabbi read from Leviticus. He explained how the people of Israel had been instructed to offer a sacrifice of twelve loaves of challah to God every Sabbath.

That night, Esperanza couldn't sleep. She kept thinking how she needed to show God how grateful she was to be able to live freely as a Jew. She tossed and turned until she had an idea—she would bake twelve loaves of challah and place them in the Holy Ark before Shabbat.

The following week, on Friday morning, Esperanza baked twelve loaves of challah. As she worked the dough, she kneaded in her desire to fulfill the *mitzvot*, the commandments, and to be a good person. She wrapped the loaves in cloth, and in the afternoon, well before sundown, she snuck into the synagogue. She had to be careful not to be seen because women weren't allowed to open the Ark. She entered quietly, opened it, and put her twelve loaves inside.

Shortly after she left, a man named Itzhak entered the sanctuary. He had once been a merchant, but a few months prior, the ship carrying his goods sank in a storm, and he lost everything. The rabbi offered Itzhak the position of caretaker for the synagogue, and while Itzhak was grateful for the position, it didn't earn him enough to feed his rather large family.

Itzhak stood in front of the Ark. "Holy One, please help me feed my family."

Then he opened the Ark, as he always did before the Sabbath, so he could dust around the Torah. To his astonishment, along with the Torah, he found twelve objects wrapped in cloth nestled inside. At first, he was appalled. But when he removed the wrappings, the scent of baked bread filled his nostrils, and his empty stomach grumbled.

"It's a miracle," Itzhak said. "Thank you, Lord!" He took a loaf of challah home to feed his young family and gave the others away to families he knew were as hungry as his.

During Shabbat services, the rabbi opened the Ark. Esperanza stood on her tiptoes so she could see inside. The bread was gone! God had accepted her gift.

Every week afterward, Esperanza baked challah and placed it inside the Ark before services. And every time the rabbi opened the Ark, the bread was gone. This went on for months.

One Friday morning, almost a full year since Esperanza first started leaving challah in the Ark, Esperanza's friend Shayna couldn't find her glasses. All week she had looked for them. In her bedroom. In her kitchen. Even under the books stacked in her sitting room. They were nowhere in her house. Then she realized that she must have left them in the synagogue. That Friday afternoon, she went to the women's loft in the synagogue, and there, under her usual seat, she found her glasses. When she stood up in triumph, she saw the strangest sight—Esperanza placing something inside the Ark.

"What are you doing?" Shayna asked. "You're not allowed there."

"I'm giving my weekly gift to God," Esperanza said.

She told Shayna the whole story of the twelve loaves. Shayna was stunned. God didn't eat bread. Yet, Esperanza was never one to lie. There had to be a reason the bread disappeared every week.

"Let's hide and see what happens," Shayna said.

Esperanza joined Shayna upstairs, and the two ladies peered over the banister. Moments later, they saw Itzhak open the Ark and take the challah.

"Thank you, Lord, for feeding my family," Itzhak said.

Shayna laughed. "You are right, Itzhak," she called down to him. "The Lord has been providing for you, but not in the way you think." She put her hand on Esperanza's shoulder. "You were right, too, my dear friend. You have been giving God weekly gifts, for it is a mitzvah to help those in need. Itzhak, it was for her love of God that Esperanza has been providing your family with food. Perhaps, though, from now on, she can give the challah directly to you and the other families."

Esperanza continued to bake twelve loaves of challah every week, but after that day, she delivered them herself to the homes of hungry families, stopping at Itzhak's first. She did this for years, never asking for help because she enjoyed baking challah. Eventually, the arthritis in her hands became so bad that she could no longer knead and braid the dough. Esperanza cried. How would she be able to make her gift for God and help feed families in need? At that moment, Adara, Itzhak's oldest daughter, now grown into a young lady, came to visit.

"I have come to ask for one more gift, Esperanza," she said.

"I don't know what I can give. My hands have betrayed me. They no longer can make bread."

Adara smiled. "Teach me to bake challah so that I can carry on your tradition."

Esperanza taught her how to mix the dough, how to knead it and let it sit to rise, and how to braid it before baking. Adara was a good student, and before long she was making challah as sweet and tender as Esperanza's. And every week from that day forward, Adara baked twelve loaves of challah. She wrapped the loaves in cloth and delivered them to the homes of families in need, stopping at Esperanza's last. Esperanza always greeted her with a smile and invited her in. The two ladies would then sit in Esperanza's kitchen, drinking tea and enjoying each other's company.

ABOUT THE STORY

Food plays an important role in Jewish holidays, especially challah, a braided bread that we eat every Shabbat and on the high holidays. Many *maggidim* have told versions of this story, which originated hundreds of years ago in Palestine. It has been published often, under different titles. Syd Lieberman published it as "Challahs in the Ark" in *Because God Loves Stories: An Anthology of Jewish Storytelling*, edited by Steve Zeitlin. Edward M. Feinstein, Laney Katz Becker, and Howard Schwartz have also published it under that title. Lawrence Kushner titled his version "The Hands of God" in his *The Book of Miracles*. I first read this story in Seymour Rossel's story collection, *The Essential Jewish Stories: God, Torah, Israel and Faith*, in which he titled it "Twelve Loaves." I have made many adaptations to the story. In my version, Esperanza, the wife, takes the leading role, and I changed the ending by introducing a new character, the caretaker's daughter.

Bella's Beautiful Coat

DEBORAH ROSENBERG

IN THE fall after she finished her studies, Bella's favorite grandma bought her a beautiful new coat.

"You will need this coat to start your grown-up life. I hope you have it forever!" Grandma said as she helped Bella put it on.

After thanking and kissing her grandma, Bella ran to the seamstress shop where her best friend, Fanny Ida, worked with her mother.

"It is beautiful indeed," Fanny Ida said as she felt along the perfect seams and checked the hang of the lining inside. "It's the loveliest coat I have seen!"

The friends stood together in front of the long mirror to admire the coat. As usual, they both talked at once.

"I love the color. That soft green plaid. It's the color of the hills in early spring."

"Yes, with the blue threads woven through? Like the color of the sky in summer."

"The fabric is as fine and soft as kittens. With a lining smooth as silk."

"And the length! It will keep you warm when fall blows cold."

"Did you feel the pockets? My coins and candies will snuggle deep and never want to leave."

As they laughed together into the mirror, Bella could just see the reflection of Fanny Ida's older brother peeking out of the back room where the sewing machines hummed. He was smiling directly at her. Suddenly her new coat felt even warmer. He stepped out and cleared his throat.

"Bella, I wonder if you'd like to walk with me in the park this afternoon, I mean, to try out your new coat?"

Fanny Ida turned and gaped at her brother. "Well, Isaac. What's this?"

Bella smiled back at Isaac and said, "I'd love to." She winked at her best friend, who giggled.

And so they did. Bella and Isaac and often Fanny Ida took walks together all that fall and well into the winter, with Bella wearing her beautiful coat. The two girls frequently talked at once, and Isaac smiled and patiently waited his turn.

Bella was wearing the coat on a cold afternoon in early spring when Isaac pulled off his mitten and took her hand, gently pulling off her mitten. When their warm hands were nestled together, Isaac said, "Bella, I love you. Will you marry me?"

Bella smiled at Isaac and said, "Isaac, I love you. I will!"

And so they married and took a little house near the shops, and time moved along through the seasons. Fanny Ida took over the seamstress shop when her mother's eyes grew tired. Bella taught school and each day made her pupils laugh and learn. Isaac wrote for the newspaper and often went on small adventures for story interviews. In time, two children were born and were named Benjamin and Dora for their grandparents.

Bella and Dora were stepping out for ice cream on Dora's eleventh birthday when Dora said to her mother, "Mama, your coat is looking a bit shabby. The hem is frayed, and that borscht stain never came out of the back. Maybe it's time for a new coat."

"Goodness, you're right. I had not noticed. But I love this coat. I wore it on my first walk with your papa. I had it on when he proposed. Perhaps your aunt Fanny Ida can help."

So Bella went to the seamstress shop to consult with her best friend.

After tea and babka and an hour of laughter, gossip, and stories, Fanny Ida inspected the coat.

"Yes, the edges are worn, on the hem and the cuffs, but the rest of the coat is fine. How about I make some alterations? We shorten here and here and make new cuffs out of a bit of velvet, and your coat becomes a smart new jacket! You can help if you like. It will be fun!"

And so they did. They worked and laughed and made a jacket.

Bella wore her smart new jacket to take Benjamin for his first day of yeshiva upper school.

She wore the jacket on countless walks with Isaac and the growing children. Bella wore the jacket to hear concerts in the park and to play chess in the square. Seasons passed.

One day, Bella was strolling through the square with Fanny Ida on their way to lunch. The friends were arm in arm when Fanny Ida glanced down and said, "Bella, your jacket is starting to unravel. See the wool here on the sleeves?"

"Oh no!" said Bella. "Is there anything you can do?"

After their lunch, Bella and Fanny Ida returned to the seamstress shop. Again, the jacket was carefully inspected. Finally, Fanny Ida announced her plan.

"Bella, I can make your jacket into a vest. We take off the sleeves, bind the armscyes. We'd take off the tall collar and revers and make a small round neckline instead. We can use some of the extra fabric to cover new buttons so they match the vest, and we can make welt pockets in the vest so you can still keep a few coins and candies. You can help!"

And so they did. They worked and laughed and made a vest.

It was a fine vest. The glorious wool was just as soft as spring green hills, and the blue threads still summoned thoughts of a summer sky. Bella wore that vest to both children's graduations. She wore that vest the first time she and Isaac met Moishe's parents, Dora's intended. Bella happened to be wearing her vest when Benjamin announced that he and Rachel were engaged. Babies were born, and the seasons passed.

One day, Bella had just put her vest on to rake the leaves that were piling up by the front door. She leaned forward with the rake and heard a quiet, awful sound. She dropped the rake and reached behind her back. The fabric across her back had torn from her shoulder to her waist. The vest had given its all.

Without changing, Bella ran to the seamstress shop. She was amazed to find herself weeping.

"What's happened?" cried Fanny Ida. "Isaac? The children? Are you hurt?"

"My vest is torn. It's ruined. I was raking … I shouldn't have put it on!"

"Oh no, it's not your fault. Fabric only lasts so long. This vest was a jacket, remember. That jacket had been a coat. You and your coat have spent a lifetime together!"

"Is there anything you can do?" Bella sobbed, as she slowly removed the torn vest.

Fanny Ida took and held it gently. She turned it this way and that. She shook her head. "There is not much stable fabric left. That coat has had a good life. Tell you what I can do; I can take what's left and make you a set of five buttons. We can sew them to anything you wish."

And so they did. They worked and laughed and made five beautiful buttons, green like the hills in early spring with a bit of blue of the summer sky. The wool was still as soft as kittens.

Bella sewed those buttons on her second favorite jacket. She proudly wore those buttons to her grandson's bar mitzvah. It was after the ceremony, when the Torah portion had been chanted, the week's teaching had been given, and the blessings were made, that the dancing began. It was quite a celebration! Bella danced with her son; she danced with her grandson. She danced with her daughter and her daughter's handsome husband. She danced with her granddaughter, and she danced with Fanny Ida. Finally, she danced with her husband Isaac, and they murmured together on the happiness that surrounded their entire family that day.

Later, once they had gone home and started getting ready for bed, Bella realized that all the buttons she'd sewn on her second favorite jacket were gone. Had she sewn them poorly? Had she danced too wildly? Whatever the reason, all the buttons were lost. Bella decided to cope with the loss in the morning; the day had been too joyous to consider sadness now.

The next morning, after breakfast, Bella kissed Isaac and again walked to the seamstress shop to see her best friend. "Fanny Ida!" she said. "All my buttons are gone. I don't know how and I don't know where or even when they disappeared. What do I do now?"

"Gone?" Fanny Ida said. "Gone with no trace?"

"Gone."

Fanny Ida sighed and went to make the tea and cut two slices of babka. The old friends sat in silence for a time, together mourning the loss of the buttons, the last of the beautiful coat.

After a time, Fanny Ida took a sip of tea and suddenly began to laugh.

"What's so funny!" demanded Bella.

Fanny Ida wiped her eyes. "I just realized ... Didn't you say your grandma said she wanted you to have that beautiful coat forever?"

"Yes, she did. But I don't. I had a coat. I loved that coat. Then thanks to you, I had a jacket. I loved that jacket. I had a vest. I loved that vest. I tore it. Then, again, thanks again to you, I had five sweet buttons. I lost them. Now, I have nothing. Nothing at all."

"Oh, my friend," replied Fanny Ida. "You have so much more than nothing. You have spent a lifetime—our friendship, your marriage, our family, your children, your grandchildren, you and me and all the blessings of our lives are woven into the fabric of that coat. The coat may be gone, but the memories! The adventures! The joys and the sorrows and the richness of life? Your coat was there for all the events of our lives. You say you have nothing? I say you have everything. Now, you have the story of the coat that became a jacket and a vest and five perfect buttons. You have a gift that truly lasts forever; you have a story to tell for the rest of time, of the beautiful coat into which our lives were woven."

ABOUT THE STORY

I often tell stories about clothes, because of the stories our clothes tell about who we are and what matters most to us. There are many versions of this story all based on the original song of the same name. I discovered this story in a beautifully illustrated children's book titled *Joseph Had a Little Overcoat* by Simms Taback. Mr. Taback cites the Yiddish song, "I Had a Little Coat," as his inspiration for the book. I have told my version of Joseph's coat many times and adapted it here to be Bella's coat in the spirit of our project.

Chana Seeks a Treasure

DEBRA GORDON ZASLOW

LONG AGO in Poland, in the city of Cracow, there lived a woman named Chana. She lived with her husband Avrom, and their big family in a tiny, one-room hut. At the center of the hut was a pot-bellied stove where, on chilly winter evenings, the family would gather for warmth and tell stories to pass the time.

Chana was a daydreamer and often her mind would wander. When she listened to a story of a queen in a castle, she would imagine she lived in a luxurious palace. She could see herself serving huge Shabbat dinners full of delicious food and wine that she'd share with all her friends. Then she'd come back to reality, in her little home, with barely enough food to feed her family.

One night when Chana slept, she dreamed she stood before the queen's palace in Prague. She gazed at the palace as it glowed in the sunset. In the dream, she heard a voice whispering, "Chana, listen to me! Look at the bridge." She noticed there was a long bridge leading up to the palace. "Go to the palace in Prague. Climb under the bridge and dig, and there you will find a treasure!" Chana woke, startled, because the dream had seemed so real. But she knew it wasn't, so she went back to sleep.

All the next day, she tried to get the dream out of her mind, but when she went to sleep, she dreamed it again. Just like in the last dream, she stood in front of the palace, and it seemed very real.

Again, the voice spoke loudly, "Chana, do what I tell you! Go to the queen's palace in Prague. Dig under the bridge, and you'll find a treasure!" This time Chana woke her husband and told him about the dream. He said, "Go back to sleep. It's only a dream." So, she did.

The next night the dream came again, but stronger. This time the voice bellowed, "Chana, what are you waiting for? Follow your dreams and go to Prague. Dig under the bridge, and you'll find the treasure!"

The next morning, Chana packed a knapsack and said goodbye to her family. She was too poor to take a carriage or a train, so she had to walk all the way. The journey took several days, but she kept her spirits up by singing songs, reciting prayers, and telling stories in her mind. She nibbled on the little food she had brought and slept under the trees along the road.

When she finally reached the palace in Prague, she stood and stared. It looked exactly like her dream. There was the bridge leading to the shining palace, but the bridge was lined with sentries, pacing back and forth, guarding it. Chana thought, *How will I get under the bridge with all the guards there?* She stood off to the side for a while, waiting and pondering what to do. She knew she had come too far to turn back, so she decided to wait until dusk and sneak down.

As the light began to fade, Chana tiptoed toward the bridge. She glanced around and saw no sentries, so she slipped down the path that led below. She took the little shovel she had brought from her knapsack and found a spot to dig. Just as she lifted the shovel, she heard a voice ring out. "Stop! What are you doing here?" Chana jumped back and saw a tall guard towering over her.

Chana trembled as she took a deep breath. She couldn't think of anything to say, so she blurted out the truth. "I ... I ... I had a dream at home in Cracow. In the dream a voice told me to come here to the palace and dig under the bridge to find a treasure! So, I walked all the way here to find it."

Chana crouched down, closed her eyes, and prayed. She didn't know if the guard would seize her and throw her in prison or let her go. Instead, she was shocked when the guard burst into laughter. He snorted, "You walked all the way from Cracow to Prague to follow your dream?"

"I did," Chana said softly.

"If I followed my dreams, I wouldn't be here," he said, still chuckling.

"Where would you be?"

"I'd be in Cracow."

"Why would you be there?"

"Because I had a dream, too. In my dream, a voice told me to go to Cracow to the home of a woman named Chana, wife of Avrom, and look underneath her pot-bellied stove to find a treasure. But half the women in Cracow are named Chana, and many of them are married to a man named Avrom. I wouldn't wear my shoes out to follow a crazy dream. I'm sorry you've wasted your time coming here."

Chana thanked him and began her journey home.

When she arrived, she looked under her stove. Sure enough, she found the hidden treasure that had always been there. It was a treasure that would sustain her all her days.

ABOUT THE STORY

This was one of the first Jewish stories I ever heard, and it is certainly one of the most famous, with variants in several collections. Jewish folklorist Howard Schwartz says, "This well-known tale has been attributed to Rabbi Nachman of Bratslav . . . but it is most likely a folktale of medieval origin." Seymour Rossel, in *Essential Jewish Stories*, attributes it to a tale of Simcha Bunim in Martin Buber's *Tales of the Hasidim, Vol. 2: Later Masters*, and cites a much older version in *1001 Tales of the Arabian Nights*. Not surprisingly, all of the versions feature a man as the main character who journeys forth only to find the treasure within. Why not have at least one version that features a woman?

Flour in the Wind

GAIL PASTERNACK

A LONG time ago, in the days of King Solomon, a woman named Rebekah lived with her family in the port city of Jaffa.

Rebekah loved to bake bread. Kneading dough, watching it rise, and breathing in the scent of yeast made her happy. She also loved helping others, so every day, in addition to the loaf of bread that she baked for her family, she baked loaves to give to her neighbors in need.

One day, there was a knock on her door. She opened it to see a man dressed in tattered clothing. He looked bedraggled.

"Are you the one who gives bread to the poor?" he asked.

Rebekah said, "Well, um, yes, but …"

His eyes were so sad, yet kind. She had already delivered all of the loaves she had baked for her neighbors, but she couldn't say no.

She gave the man her last loaf and went to her kitchen to bake another for her family. But when she went to the pantry, she saw that her flour bag was empty. Her heart sank. She searched the shelves and found a bag of dried corn.

Her family might enjoy a nice cornbread, she thought, so she carried her bag of corn past the Jaffa seashore to the town mill. She worked the large grindstone and ground the corn into flour.

After all that labor, Rebekah was tired. Her heart was light, though, as she imagined the happy faces of her children and her husband when she served them her freshly baked cornbread.

She walked along the shore, carrying her sack of flour. With each step, the sky grew darker and darker. The wind picked up. It swirled around her and stung her cheeks. The rain fell in sheets. She forced herself forward until a gust of wind ripped the sack of flour out of her hands and blew it out to sea.

"That was for my family! What did we do to deserve to go hungry?" She screamed at the top of her lungs, yet the wind ate her words. Tears poured from her eyes, yet the rain washed them away.

Anger grew in Rebekah's chest, and her mind raced. She had heard that wise King Solomon had come to Jaffa. A shipment of timber for building a great temple was due to arrive, and the king wanted to be there to inspect it.

She marched through the rain to the town center where the king was staying, but when she arrived at the royal residence, guards stopped her.

"The king is taking no more visitors today. Come back tomorrow."

"No! I must see him today."

One guard moved forward to block her from entering, but the other guard stopped him.

"Are you Rebekah?" the second guard asked. "Are you the one I've heard of, the one who gives bread to the poor?"

"Why, yes."

"Wait here." The second guard left her at the door and went inside. He came back moments later and led Rebekah to the room King Solomon used to meet visitors.

Rebekah's heart pounded, but she stood firmly in her spot and told the king everything that had happened. "What have I done to deserve this?" she asked him when she had finished her tale.

At that moment, ten men burst into the room. Each man carried a full sack over his shoulder.

The first guard ran in after them. "Sorry, my lord. I couldn't stop them."

"What have you brought me?" King Solomon asked the men.

Each man laid his sack on the floor, and the tallest of the men stepped forward.

"These sacks of gold are for the person who saved us from certain death," he said. "King Solomon, please help us find this person."

"How did this person save you?"

"We were sailing towards Jaffa when a storm came. Our ship was blown into the rocks and tore a hole in its hull. Water rushed in, and we started to sink. Just then a sack of flour came from nowhere. Water mixed with the flour, creating a ball of dough that plugged the hole. We didn't sink and were able to get to shore." He held up a sack of wet dough. "This saved us!"

Rebekah stared at the soggy sack, which dripped seawater onto the floor. "It saved you?" Her voice came out as a whisper.

King Solomon took the sack from the man. "Is this yours, Rebekah?"

"If it is, my name would be on it."

King Solomon searched and found her name embroidered into the burlap. "Then it is you who deserves this reward."

"Me? But ..." Rebekah couldn't think straight. How could this be happening?

The men picked up their sacks of gold and escorted her home. All the while, Rebekah marveled over this strange twist of fate and debated whether she should refuse their reward. The men left the gold in her parlor and bade her farewell, and as Rebekah watched them leave, she came up with a plan—she would use the money to open a bakery dedicated to feeding the poor.

Chances are, none of us will receive sacks of gold for our small acts of kindness. Nor may we ever know the ultimate results of those acts. Kindness is like the sack of flour in the wind. We have no idea where it will take us, but it doesn't matter where it takes us. What matters is that we have a chance to touch the lives of others.

ABOUT THE STORY

Many versions of this story have been told over the years. In some, the person who loses the sack of flour is a man. In others, a woman. The female version of this story by Barbara Diamond Goldin can be found in *A Child's Book of Midrash: 52 Jewish Stories from the Sages*. I first read it in Peninnah Schram's *The Hungry Clothes and Other Jewish Folktales*. When I tell this story, I like to get into Rebekah's head, exploring what she thinks and how she interacts with her setting and the characters she meets.

From Feather to Feather

CASSANDRA SAGAN

THIS STORY begins with a feather.
A tickle. A giggle. A *bissell* (just a little bit) of joy.
Esther lived for those moments when she made someone laugh. She would laugh along until her belly ached. She baked until her hair was full of flour and her kitchen smelled like heaven, and the neighborhood children filled her apartment each day after school for cookies, milk, and stories. Stories that Esther milked from them. "Did your father find a new job? How late did you say that your mama sleeps? Your aunts and uncles, cousins and neighbors, *nu*, what are they up to? What happened at the dinner table, what was in the mail?"

Esther always had a huge pot of chicken soup simmering on the stove, and when she brought bowlfuls to sick or homebound neighbors, she would regale them with embellished versions of neighborhood tales. She told her tales in the market, at the butcher's, even in the women's section at *shul*. Why not? Esther believed that laughter was as healing as drinking guggle-muggle or eating raw onions and honey.

If she heard about a leaky roof at the Bernstein's, she might say: "Did you hear? So much rain poured through their ceiling, they had to evacuate in an ark like Noah!" Or "Bessie Horowitz put so much pepper in the kugel, Bernie sneezed until his hair fell out. Now he's bald as a potato."

One day over gingersnaps, young Irwin told Esther that his mama, Mimi, a widow who earned a living baking dozens of challahs every Friday, had found ants in a batch of dough, and instead of throwing it away had baked a tiny person for him to play with.

The story twisted and wriggled and slid further from the truth each time Esther told it. The story grew legs, racing off in ten directions, told and retold by people who didn't know Esther and her playful exaggerations. "You think those are raisins and poppy seeds in Mimi's challah? Look again. If ants land in the batter, she bakes them in for extra crunch."

Customers began canceling their challah orders. Mimi was devastated. Esther was mortified. She had to find a way to undo the harm she had caused Mimi. So she headed over to seek the advice of Sarah, a wise woman whom Esther trusted with all her heart.

"Sarah, *oy oy oy*! I've done something terrible, and I need your help. I have to make this right." And she told Sarah the whole story, without exaggeration.

Sarah listened, deep in thought. After a few minutes, she said, "Esther, do you have a feather pillow?"

Esther patted her bottom, and said, "No, that's my *tukhis*."

Sarah frowned. Esther shook her head. "Ach, I'm sorry. It's this kind of joking that got poor Mimi into this mess. Yes, of course I have a feather pillow."

"Get your pillow and meet me on the synagogue roof in half an hour."

Esther hurried home and got the pillow. Leaning forward she climbed the four flights of stairs to reach the roof. In tears, she blubbered, "I've got to make this right."

Sarah led Esther to the low wall at the corner of the roof. She reached into her pocket and pulled out a pair of sewing scissors, handing them to Esther. "Cut the pillow open, then shake it until every single feather is released."

It was a breezy day, leaves rustling above and banners flapping below. Esther vigorously shook out her pillow, watching the feathers fly up and over the wall, catching in branches, between buildings, landing in the gutter, floating onto the tops of taxis and between the spokes of bicycle wheels. She turned to Sarah, eyebrows raised. "Is that it? Did I make it right?"

Sarah shook her head sadly. "There's one more step. Now you must gather every single feather and put them back into the pillow."

Gesturing frantically at the far-flung feathers fanning across the neighborhood, Esther cried, "But no one can possibly do that!"

Sarah nodded. "You're right. No one can. And in the same way, we can never take back our *lashon hara*, our evil tongue, our careless, hurtful words. Once rumors and gossip leave your lips, they travel like feathers on the wind, and you can never take them back."

Esther took a deep breath, tears falling from her eyes. It was a difficult lesson, but from that day forward she strove to be more careful with every word that left her lips.

This is where the original story, told about the nineteenth-century Polish rabbi known as the Chofetz Chaim, ends. While it is true that, like Esther, we can never take back our false and hurtful words, I've learned that it is also true that we can never take back our words of praise or blessing either. Our acts of lovingkindness, our *mitzvot*, spread like feathers in every direction, and we may never know where they land or who they touch. Sometimes the blessings remain hidden for generations.

My Nana is a perfect example. She was a conduit for blessing. Saturday nights we danced polkas in our pajamas to the music of Lawrence Welk and sang along with Mitch Miller before bed. Chirping off-key lullabies, Nana perched on the edge of the bed like a bird. Then she would turn off the lamp, kiss me on my *keppe*, and stand at the foot of my bed, lifting the blue blanket gently into the air. My covers seemed to hover then drift to the bed in slow motion,

Nana's face rising above like a moon. I felt safe and loved, blessed and tickled, connected to the source of light and life.

Many years later I learned about an Ashkenazi tradition where mothers would recite the bedtime *Shema* while lifting a feather quilt into the air and letting it fall slowly to the bed.

I began to sob so hard that I could barely breathe.

Nana was one thousand percent Jewish. She never ate pork or shellfish or had a gentile friend in her life. But she was not religious. She never said the bedtime Shema with us; she might not have even known that it existed. Yet I know in my kishkes, deep in my guts, that long ago, her mother, or grandmother, or great-great-great-ancestor, put her children to sleep while lifting the blanket and reciting the bedtime Shema. Over time, the words of the prayer were buried deep within the ritual, but their essence had never been lost. In that very moment, the love and blessings of generations of my ancestors drifted down upon me like feathers, gifts that had been hidden for lifetimes in plain sight.

Shema	My Nana
Yisrael	lifted the feather quilt
YHVH	by the corners
Elohaynu	and let it float
YHVH	through the air
Echad	to my bed

Baruch shem kavod malchuto l'olam vaed.

ABOUT THE STORY

Many stories have been written about the Lithuanian Rabbi Israel Meir Kagan, known as the Chofetz Chaim, and his legendary wisdom and kindness. This story about the feather pillow has been told and retold dozens of times, but in every case, there is a male rabbi who teaches the penitent a lesson. It was imperative for me to tell this story through a female lens, and to take it a step further to include our *lashon tov*, our good words and actions, spreading unstoppably, continuously, *l'dor v'dor*, across the generations. The Shema is a key declaration of faith in Judaism, often translated as, "Hear O Israel, The Lord, our god, the Lord is one." The line that follows, which is often translated as "Blessed be His Name and His glorious kingdom, forever and ever," is usually whispered.

Emptying Cups

GAIL PASTERNACK

"Jews call their bible the Pentateuch," the woman serving me tea said.

This was about twenty years ago. The woman's name was Virginia, and she was the mother of one of my son's friends. I had met her several times at play groups, but this was the first time I had visited her home in Irvington, a well-established neighborhood in northeast Portland. We were sitting in her Craftsman-style living room on white couches in front of a stone-hearth fireplace.

"Do you mean the Torah?" I asked as I took my cup from her.

"I haven't read much of the Old Testament ... the Pentateuch. Sorry." She gave me a sheepish smile. "Anyway, my priest has been teaching us all about Judaism lately. It's fascinating." She sat on the edge of the couch. "He told us that the Jewish name for God is Yah Wah."

I thought, *That's news to me.*

Up until then, I had never heard that name. No Jewish person I had ever met had used it. But I figured that since I was a Hebrew school dropout, I probably hadn't heard of many things.

She then explained why it was so important to serve round challah bread on all Jewish holidays.

"Um, we only serve round—"

"And the braids represent the three patriarchs."

As she continued to talk about my religion, I browsed the books on the shelves flanking the fireplace. Most were theology books.

Virginia has no interest in what I have to say about my own religion, I thought. *She just wants to prove to me how much she knows.* I clasped my teacup and recalled a story that I had recently read to my children. A Zen story that goes like this ...

Long ago, there was a student who wanted to know everything about Zen philosophy and practice. He read everything he could but still felt he didn't know enough, so he went to the home of a great Zen master and knocked on the door. "Master, please teach me everything you know. I promise to be a good student," he said.

"Come in. Let me serve you tea."

And as the master prepared the tea, the student tried to prove how worthy he was of instruction. He told the master everything he had read.

"I know all about the *zazen* posture. It's vital to sit with your left foot on your right thigh and your right foot on your left in the perfect lotus position. It is the expression of duality."

On and on the student talked.

The master handed the young man a teacup and began to pour. And as the student spoke, the master poured tea into the cup.

Up to the rim. He kept pouring.

The tea spilled over into the saucer. He kept pouring.

The tea spilled over the rim of the saucer and onto the floor. But the master kept pouring.

"Stop," the student cried. "The cup is full."

"Yes, your cup is full," the master said. "You know all the answers, so how can I teach you more? Come back to me when your cup is empty, and then I will be able to teach you."

After having tea with Virginia, I realized that I regretted dropping out of Hebrew school and I needed to learn more about Judaism. I enrolled in a local congregation, I read books, and I studied Hebrew and the art of Jewish storytelling. During my *maggid* training, I made an amazing discovery about the connection between words and emptiness. It all starts in the beginning, in *Bereshet*, the first book of the Torah.

At first there is emptiness, and then God speaks the world into existence. His words become things, the things of the universe. The Hebrew verb for "to speak," *dahbere*, also means "word" or "thing." There is a connection between the two.

Interestingly, the same root may be found in the word for "wilderness," *midbar*, which was where the Israelites received the word of God, the Torah. The wilderness, a place void of all the things of man. An empty place.

Like my friend Virginia, I too often assume I know things about other people. Many of us do. Sometimes we like other people based on what we think we know. Sometimes we don't like them. Either way, we are allowing prejudgments to dictate our beliefs and behaviors. Yet, if we want to live in peace with each other, we need to empty our cups of our preconceptions and open our minds.

When we tell a story, we immerse our listeners into another world, and this separation from everyday life allows listeners to lower their guards. Then when we present the world of the story from the point of view of our characters, listeners see things from a different perspective.

Maggidim empty the cups of preconceptions and prejudice, leaving listeners open and ready to learn. That's our superpower. Through our stories, we can return listeners to the barren wilderness, the empty place where we receive the word of God.

ABOUT THE STORY

Maggidim often combine a story with a teaching, and sometimes they combine a classic story with a personal story. I do both here by blending a personal story with a teaching from the Torah and an ancient Zen parable called "Empty Your Cup." This parable dates back to either the late eighth century or early ninth century. I first heard it when I studied karate in New York City in the 1980s. This small story had a huge impact on me. Not only did it teach me that prejudice gets in the way of learning, it also taught me the power of story. Years later, I read "Empty-Cup Mind" in Heather Forest's book, *Wisdom Tales from Around the World*, which compiles stories from many cultures. During my maggidah training, when I saw the similarities between Jewish teachings and this Zen parable, I was inspired to blend them with my personal story.

PART FIVE
Torah Women

They Will Call Me Naamah

BATYA PODOS

WELL, HERE we are, starting all over again. I never agreed to this, you know. I miss my garden, my neighbors, everything familiar. Although, it's good to get the stench of animals out of my nostrils. That's one good thing. Noah's planting a vineyard. He's always loved his wine.

I remember exactly when my husband began having private conversations with God, when everything changed. He became distracted and went about muttering to himself. He and our sons would huddle together speaking in urgent whispers. He didn't tell me what they spoke about or what he and God were planning. Off they went to cut down trees and gather materials.

Noah had always been reliable, even a little dull, but that suited me fine. I like dull. I like the predictability of knowing what will happen each day. I love planting my garden, watching for the first shoots, then the harvest and the feast. It has a pattern to it. But this wasn't a part of any pattern I'd known.

And God didn't just speak to my husband. When I asked Noah how he knew what to do, he told me God put the plans in his head. When I asked about them, he told me in too much detail: measurements by cubits, materials of cypress wood and pitch, and a hundred other things. We are not a seafaring people. As far as I know,

Noah had never even been on a boat, and he certainly had no idea how to build one, so he needed all the help he could get.

Did I say boat? This was no boat; it was huge, enormous. And suddenly, it was in my front garden, growing bigger every day. Gone were my tomatoes, my cucumbers, my melons. My husband was obsessed. He hardly spoke to me anymore, just to God. I wished God had put a few other things in Noah's head. I missed my husband.

The neighbors came over to watch. They thought Noah had gone mad. I didn't say anything, but I agreed. He wasn't young, you know. Maybe this was some kind of midlife crisis. Whatever it was, this ark took over his life, mine too, and I had no way to stop it.

One night, after a day of building, Noah told me that God was going to send a great flood and destroy everything, and that we were the only ones who would be left alive. "What's the matter with you?" I asked him. "God talks to you—don't you talk back? What about our neighbors, our friends? What about their children? Why don't you speak up for them? Change God's mind?" But Noah said nothing. Not to me, and apparently not to God.

Thinking about it now, my heart still breaks. I know God doesn't speak to me, and if there is ever a chronicle of this, no one will remember my name. But if I could speak to God, I would give a piece of my mind. I would say, "Why don't you have patience with your own creation? Why can't you be kinder and more forgiving? We can all learn to be better with a little encouragement. Ask me—I'm a mother; I know how to deal with children. But no—God has to destroy the whole thing. My garden was gone, nothing but mud, thanks to the rain that began without stop.

Once the ark was finished, the animals came. They just arrived, ready to board. It was eerie. Lions and antelope standing together. We were supposed to live on the ark with these creatures. Noah and me, our sons and their wives, my daughters-in-law. No one will remember their names either. And then, suddenly, it was time. I was barely able to gather my seeds and seedlings when we were hustled onto the ark and the hatch was closed. Then, it was just us and the animals, waiting.

It kept raining. Our neighbors packed up and moved to higher ground, but Noah said it would do them no good. I couldn't bear to watch them drown. I've known them for so many years, exchanged remedies for a cough, shared the garden's bounty, looked after each other's children. Maybe in God's eyes, they had done wrong, but not in mine. I'm sure if given a chance, they would have repented. But there was no chance. Not for them. What makes me better than they are? Why wasn't I left to drown?

Through the portholes Noah had built into the ark, I watched the waters cover everything and everyone I knew. The water lifted us up and set us floating out onto this new sea. There was nothing but water, above and below. I cried for days, adding my tears to the water. I would like to think that God cried too, that God's tears of grief and sorrow and loss made that endless sea our home. To be the only ones left is a terrible thing, maybe as terrible as drowning.

We were stuck with each other and the animals for one hundred fifty days. I know because I counted each one. It stank on the ark, no matter how much mucking out we did. It was the worst of barnyard, stable, and midden all combined. And after a while, we could barely stand to be in each other's company.

Noah didn't touch me once we boarded the ark, hardly spoke to me. I was invisible. I'm his wife, but I didn't exist. My only comfort was the animals, despite the stink. So, I went into the belly of the ark where the beasts and birds lay together, and I would stroke them and sing to them. And they responded to me. When I think of it now, a terrible longing takes me, as it did then. I think of the Garden that God created at the beginning of time, when we could be one with the animals. I don't eat their flesh anymore. I looked into their eyes and saw myself.

After all those days of rain, the wind came up, and we found ourselves on the top of a mountain with the water receding beneath us. It was the new moon, and my daughters—the wives of my sons—and I celebrated this occasion, the landing of our craft combined with the sweet new moon. We combed and braided each other's hair, we dressed up in what finery we had left, we took each other's hands, and we danced and sang.

The next day, Noah asked for birds. I brought him a raven, its heart trembling against its chest as I held it in my hands. Noah took it from me and threw it up into the air. In my mind, I flew with it. I was the raven. I was also the dove, sent out over the water. And when one returned with a branch in its beak, I knew the ordeal was over, but another one would take its place. How do you build a life when everything you know is gone? Where do you begin?

And when the land was dry and the animals released into this new world, there was a bow of color in the sky. A rainbow. The colors dazzled me after so many days in the ark. I wanted to feel hopeful. Noah said God had blessed him and our sons and made a covenant with him to never bring a flood again. The rainbow was pretty, but where was my blessing? And the blessings for my daughters, the wives of my sons? Where is my covenant? God doesn't speak to me. But it doesn't matter because I have my own covenant in the seeds in my pockets, the seedlings I nursed to keep alive all that time in the ark. My covenant is in the rebuilding and renewal.

In years ahead, when you look for me, I will be called Naamah, a name they'll give me for my drumming and singing. They will say I sang for idols, that I beat my drum for them in worship, but that is a lie. I'll sing and play for God, like my sisters before me, but our God understands that sometimes people struggle to find the light within themselves, that we can so easily be attracted to things that harm us. So, our God has patience, forbearance, kindness, and compassion.

We are always afloat on the waters, the whole of our lives like a ship, never quite sure where we will land. Most of us manage to stay afloat until we reach our uncertain destinations. And what do we do when we finally find ourselves on dry land? We begin again as best we can. We are resilient. We keep to our own truths. And sometimes, we watch for rainbows, and we hope.

ABOUT THE STORY

There have been many midrashim written about Naamah, Noah's wife. This original story was meant to be a gift for Maggidah Melissa Carpenter, whose Torah monologues have inspired me for many years. But when I began teaching Torah to young students, I realized it echoes their questions, so now this story is a gift for them too. After my students learn about the flood, they always respond the same: God is mean, God isn't fair, God can't be trusted. We all wrestle with the shadow side of Torah. This story, I hope, reflects some of that from a woman's point of view.

Serach bat-Asher, the Story

JOSÉ DE KWAADSTENIET

If **Serach** bat-Asher were a man, you may have known her story before now.

Her story begins when a famine was going on in Canaan, and Jacob's sons traveled to Egypt to buy grain—the country where the granaries were still packed. There they met the viceroy, their brother Joseph, whom they had dumped some twenty years before—Joseph, who ended up in Egypt and through a series of coincidences had become the confidante of Pharaoh. Though the brothers didn't recognize him at first, all's well that ends well, as they were finally reunited. There was a small problem though.

Reuben, Jacob's eldest son, asked his brothers, "How are we going to tell Dad that Joseph is still alive? If we tell him upfront ... well, I'm afraid his heart may fail." Asher thought for a moment, then said, "You know, Dad adores Serach, my daughter. Why don't we ask her to tell her grandfather?"

Serach, Asher's daughter.

You might never have heard of her, but there she is, in chapter forty-six of Genesis which says, "These are the names of the sons of Israel/Jacob who came to Egypt ..." And then: "The sons of Asher are ... and their sister Serach." A daughter, a sister, a granddaughter!

Serach. Young, buoyant; a full head of dark hair, dark sparkling eyes. She could play melodies on her harp—so sweet that even the angels would stop their chores to listen. She wove the most beautiful garments and tapestries with breathtaking patterns and colors. And those eyes—they seemed to see right through you; it was as if Serach was able to see ... to see what exactly?

Either way, it was decided: Asher went to his daughter and asked her to tell her *sabba* (grandfather) that Joseph was still alive. Serach thought for a moment and said, "Okay, I'll do it, on one condition though: I will tell him in my own way." And so, it was agreed.

The next morning Serach wrapped herself in her multicolored shawl, took her harp, and went to Jacob at the hour that she knew he would be *davening*, praying his morning prayers. She entered the room. Her grandfather stood there, rocking back and forth, back and forth, his hand before his eyes. She waited for a minute, and then she started to play her harp—very softly, with an alluring melody as she sought to adjust her playing to her granddad's singing. Jacob caught his breath for a fraction of a second.

After a few minutes, she started to hum, and eventually she sang sweetly, softly but clearly:

"Joseph is in Egypt; he is alive.

Your grandsons: hear me, they thrive!

Efraim and Manasseh—dear Sabba: there's new life ... "

She sang and she sang, melodiously reaching out to her grandfather—and then she realized: *He knows. Sabba knows. He heard me.*

In fact, Jacob was in turmoil. He buried his face in his hands and mumbled, "I don't feel well; I don't feel well at all! I think I'm going to faint." But he didn't; he went on praying his closing prayers, and suddenly he knew—really knew—that, indeed, Joseph was alive!

After he finished his prayers, Jacob looked at his beloved granddaughter, and it was as if he saw her for the first time—with those piercing eyes and that multicolored shawl wrapped around her shoulders.

With tears streaming down his face, he hugged Serach and said, "Sweetheart, you gave me back my life. And while I was praying, I suddenly knew for sure: because you are a giver of life, death won't be able to get a grip on you ever."

Impossible! Serach thought, *No idea what grandpa is talking about.* She would find out all right, although it would take some time.

Actually, it would take centuries before we meet her again. As a matter of fact, at the end of Numbers, chapter twenty-six, when we are told that Moses carried out a census as the people were on the verge of entering the Promised Land, there she is again, Serach bat-Asher! Why here? And how is this possible, after more than four centuries? There has to be a reason.

Imagine. At some point Joseph died. On his deathbed, he had made his family promise that when they would return to Canaan they would take him with them. But of course, after more than four hundred years, the question was: Who remembered where Joseph was buried?!

Let's dive into the Talmud and have a closer look.

The Israelites were packed and ready: ready to leave Egypt, but where was Moses? Well, Moses was searching the surroundings for Joseph's grave, wandering about, muttering, "Now where could that grave be?"

Miriam, Moses' sister, clever as always, got a brilliant idea and went to her very old, wise and flamboyant "aunt" Serach, with her gray curls and those sparkling eyes that looked right through you. Nobody knew her age—she seemed to have been there always.

Miriam said to her, "Aunt Serach, my brother went searching for Joseph's grave. Now, I wondered, do you have an inkling where he might be buried?"

Serach said, "My child, why didn't Moses ask me right away? Of course I know! Let that boy come to me. I'll tell him."

Miriam went after Moses and brought him to Serach.

Serach said to Moses, "A long story short: The Egyptians put his bones in a lead coffin and let it sink into the Nile. You know why? I'll tell you. Thanks to Joseph, Egypt had grain in abundance during that great famine. Now, the Egyptians were hoping that Joseph's bones would be a blessing for the Nile, so that the river would give its fertility in the same abundance as during Joseph's life. So there he is, in the Nile."

Moses said, "Oh. Great. How on earth are we getting Joseph out of the water?"

Serach said, "Easy enough. Call him."

Moses grimaced, thinking, *Of course, call him. Why didn't I think of it? Oh well, what have we got to lose?*

So he went to the riverside and shouted, "Joseph, if you want to come with us, you'll have to surface now. Otherwise, we'll leave without you!" And lo and behold: the coffin came to the surface!

Serach bat-Asher. She is the connecting link between Jacob and Joseph, and between Joseph and Moses. Reaching out over centuries, in mysterious ways. Don't forget her. An indispensable woman, one of a kind.

She is not the only one in Torah too easily forgotten, too rarely seen: Sarah, Rebecca, Leah, and Rachel. And don't forget Tamar. Oh, and there is Deborah. To name a few. And of course, those courageous women during the oppression in Egypt. Women—each and every one of them playing a crucial role at a crucial moment in our history. Reaching out over ages—in a way like Serach.

And what about us? What about me?

May we all—women known and unknown, forgotten and remembered—stretch outward over centuries and find our mysterious connections.

ABOUT THE STORY

Several years ago, I read about Serach for the first time (I can't remember where). So when our paths crossed again, I was overjoyed. That second time occurred when I read "The Chronicle of Serah Bat-Asher" in Howard Schwartz's *Gabriel's Palace*. Isn't she irresistible? For me she is. So, I closed my eyes—and in my imagination the stories about this immortal woman started to flesh out. This version is the result.

Miriam Chats with God

MELISSA CARPENTER

MY GOD, my God, why did you do this to me? One moment I'm Miriam the Prophetess—old, healthy, strong, respected. The next moment—I'm an abomination, afflicted with *tzara'at*, shedding scales of skin like drifts of snow. Unclean, unclean! Shamed and shunned, seven days outside the camp. And I've only been out here for one day. I've got six more days to get through.

Why did you do this to me, God? This itching is unbearable! No, I take that back. The itching is a temporary inconvenience, but it's all part of God's plan, and I accept it humbly.

Hhhh! Look at me now! Scaly as a snake, white as—salt. Reminds me of Lot's wife, when she looked back at Sodom burning, and she turned into a pillar of salt.

Because she looked back—

But I never look back. I always look forward, because I have faith in you, God. Whenever the men whine about the cucumbers and melons and leeks and onions and garlic they used to eat in Egypt, what do I do? I invent another recipe for manna.

And when we left Egypt, grabbing whatever we could, I packed my timbrel. Because I knew we'd have a reason to celebrate. Even when the Pharaoh's chariots came after us, I knew sooner or later we'd be singing and dancing and praising you, God.

I bet you didn't expect an old lady to dance like that, did you?

Hey, I was forward-looking even when I was young, before Moses was born. Remember when Pharaoh ordered the Egyptians to drown every Hebrew baby boy? How my father, Amram, told the other Hebrew men to separate from their wives? He said it's better not to make a baby at all, than to see him drowned in the Nile.

But I said, "What about the girl babies?" I said, "I had a vision about a boy who escaped." I said, "Someday God's gonna hear our groaning and rescue us." I said, "In the meantime, let's grab as much life as we can, even under the shadow of death." I said, "You should tell all the married men to go back to their wives' beds and bring some light into the night!"

And my father did just what I said. Turned out well, didn't it?

Their next baby was Moses, your prophet who led us all out of Egypt!

These days I feel sorry for that poor Cushite woman Moses married. This whole journey through the wilderness, she's been sleeping alone every night.

So I spoke up. I said, "I'm a prophet too, and so is Aaron, and we don't neglect our spouses that way." And what did you do, God? You called all three of us to the Tent of Meeting and told us Moses is a different kind of prophet. All right. But then suddenly, *hhhh!* You struck me with the skin disease *tzara'at* and I'm shedding scales all over the place. Now everyone turns away from me because I'm unclean.

But I'm not complaining. I have a good attitude. I know this is all for the best. Somehow.

One, two, three … This is day four. I'm halfway through my seven days outside the camp. Halfway through this long, long week. But I'm not complaining!

Though I still don't know why I'm being punished. Listen, I know Moses is way above my level. I mean, the man has to wear a veil over his face! Because he's been exposed to so much of your divine light, his own face glows. Me, I've just got a regular old woman's face. Or I used to, before you crusted it over with white scales.

But just because you turned my little brother into the prophet of all prophets, am I supposed to treat him like a king? Like a god? Somebody who can't be criticized?

I only wanted to make the point that even if Moses does talk with God all the time, he could still go to bed with his wife once in a while. The poor thing is shriveling up from lack of affection. My God, you give us life, you give us desire, you give us joy like fire when two people come together. Is it right to reject your gifts? Is it right for Moses to turn away from his wife? Isn't that turning away from life?

So, I told Moses he should go back to her bed, just like the men of Israel went back to their wives in Egypt. But I couldn't tell if I was getting through to him; it's hard to read his expression, through that veil. And Aaron the Eloquent just stood there like a dummy. So I kept talking. I told Moses, "Look at me and Aaron, we're prophets, too. But Aaron still gives Elisheva a kiss whenever he steps into their tent. And me, I was good to my own man, right up to the day he died."

So, God, what did I do wrong? Was it bad to say that we're prophets, too? We are. You do speak to us. You spoke to us right then, telling us to report to the Tent of Meeting. And when we got there, we heard your voice again, from the pillar of cloud, and you said plenty. All three of us heard you. And then *hhhh!* I'm covered with tzara'at. Skin like scales. Like salt. Like death. Me, not Aaron. Why me? Because I was doing the talking?

You know, God, you always did let Aaron off the hook. Like when he made the golden calf. You hold me to a higher standard. Maybe it's a compliment. Maybe this scaly skin is actually a sign of your favor. I just need to look at it the right way.

I have to confess, my good attitude has been slipping, these past four days outside the camp. I guess it's easier to keep smiling when I have people to smile at. Now that I'm alone, I—I'm starting to lose faith that you make everything work out for the best.

It must be a passing weakness. I never actually break down. I know I can get through all seven days of tzara'at with my chin up.

Hhhhh! I still can't get used to this itching! But this is the seventh day. I just have to stick it out until sunset, and it will be over.

I've got to remember to thank Moses for begging God to heal me. If it weren't for him, I'd be stuck like this for the rest of my life. Thanks to Moses, I can come back into the camp tonight and be myself again.

But it won't be the same, will it? Everyone will remember what you did to me, God. When I walked out of the camp seven days ago, nobody would meet my eyes. When I come back—I bet they won't look at me the way they used to.

Could be worse. At least I won't have to wear a veil, like Moses. Only time I ever wore a veil was for my wedding. I remember when my husband lifted the veil and kissed me.

But Moses, he only takes off his veil to talk to God, or to tell the people what God said. And they all listen to him. Nobody's going to argue with a man when his face is glowing like the sun.

Most people take one glance at his face, then look off to the side until he's done talking. You can see everyone relax when he puts the veil back on. Covering his face again is a kindness, so he won't frighten anyone.

I suppose if he wanted to kiss his wife, he'd have to kiss her through the veil. Not so easy. And their eyes can't meet, not really. But if he took off his veil, she couldn't bear to look at him at all.

I never thought of that before. Since Moses speaks face to face with you, God, that means he can't speak face to face with anyone else. Not even his wife. Nobody can look him in the face.

I wonder if he feels like he's being shunned.

I got seven days of shunning. Moses got a lifetime sentence. Poor man. Maybe that's why he's so humble.

Maybe I was wrong to criticize him for being a bad husband. His life is a lot harder than I realized. I wonder if he ever looks back on the old days in Midian, where he was just a shepherd and a family man. I wouldn't blame him.

Actually, I can't blame Lot's wife for looking back at Sodom. What good was it to escape, when her older daughters were dying in the fire and brimstone? Maybe I shouldn't even blame the Israelites for looking back on our life in Egypt as if it were a good thing. At least in Egypt there was always garlic.

Imagine, I've been so proud of not looking back! How did I get to be so old without ever turning my head around? You know, even after my husband died, I didn't let myself look back and long for him. I thought I was so important, Miriam the Prophetess, I had to set an example. I had to keep my chin up and my face toward the Promised Land every day, every moment. And I thought I was so righteous, I could tell everyone else how to behave, too.

Hah! What a stiff-necked Jew I've been.

Blessed are you, my God, who blessed me with seven days to look back.

ABOUT THE STORY

I create "Torah monologues" by imagining the thoughts of biblical characters. This monologue is based on Numbers 12:1-15, where Miriam criticizes Moses' marriage and protests that she is a prophet, too. God punishes her with a skin disease and seven days of isolation. I wondered what direction Miriam's thoughts would take during those seven days. At first, I figured she would be relentlessly positive; this is how she appears in the midrash about Miriam as a little girl in Talmud Bavli, Sotah 12a, as well as in the tradition that she anticipated the celebration in Exodus 15:20-21 and told the women to pack their drums when they left Egypt. But by the end of her week of tzara'at, Miriam might be more reflective and feel sympathy for her brother Moses—turning God's punishment into a blessing.

Tears Before the Gate

JOSÉ DE KWAADSTENIET

During the *Yamim Nora'im*, the Days of Awe, in one of the *selichot* (penitential prayers), we hear (in my own words): "Isn't it true that you hear the sound of weeping? Please! Give our tears a permanent place in that special tears-storage room of yours!" Apparently the Eternal One has a container for our tears.

I find the image moving. The Talmud formulates it a bit differently: in searching for contact with the Divine Presence, the gates of tears are never closed.

Here's the story—

Wham! With a boom the gate slammed shut behind them. There was no way back. There they stood, Adam and Eve, huddled together, scared, devastated. But above all, they regretted their stupidity with that tree, a bit earlier.

Now, fear and regret were totally new phenomena. After all, emotions were alien to them when they were in the Garden of Eden. Think of it: how can you consciously feel joy if you have no clue that the opposite of joy could exist? If everything is beautiful, good, perfect, what's the use of fear or regret?

So there they stood. The garment the Holy One had made for Eve was already torn, ripped open by the sharp point of a rock near the gate. But nothing was as sharp as the pain she and Adam felt in their hearts about their lost innocence.

They looked at each other and said, simultaneously, "What have we done?"

Now, it seemed that the Holy One had also asked herself this question, "What have I done?" because, in her inscrutable way, she suddenly appeared, right next to them.

"Hmm," she said. "Well. No way the two of you could have stayed in the Garden of Eden. Believe me! But now you are entering a world that, except that she is astonishingly beautiful, also will bring you a lot of pain and troubles. You will always be the love of my life, believe me (the Eternal One has something with belief), but the fact is that you have a lot coming. Unimaginable beauty. And unimaginable suffering—that too."

Eve and Adam looked at each other again and felt a new emotion creeping up: despair.

To see them so utterly forlorn—the Eternal One just couldn't bear it. "Hmm. Well. You know what the Yiddish *rachmones* means? Compassion. As in, you came from my *rechem*—my womb so to speak, and I can't possibly leave you out in the cold now, can I? So, I'll give you something of priceless worth. Look! This is a tear. Now, if pain becomes unbearable, tears will come from your eyes. And you will see that somehow this will give you some air, breathing space—light."

After Eve and Adam received the Eternal One's gift, there was no stopping it. Tears rolled down their faces, because of irretrievable loss and because of an unimaginable future. Their first tears. But, to their surprise, they noticed it was true: their tears broke through the gravity of their pain. Don't ask how. Somehow.

They realized something else too: their tears formed a connection with the Eternal One. They knew that their tears had found a permanent place in God's universe.

Tears are a priceless gift from the Eternal One to us. Tears render pain and sorrow transparent for light. Then the one transforms into the other—pain merging with light.

So, whichever gates will close on *Yom Kippur*: the gates of tears are never closed.

ABOUT THE STORY

One of the first compilations of Jewish stories I bought was *A Treasury of Jewish Folklore* by Nathan Ausubel. Not exactly new, but a treasury it is. "The First Tear" was one of the stories in the book that really spoke to me immediately: God showing himself from her best female side. It is that aspect that I worked out here. And then some.

PART SIX
Supernatural Stories

House of the Demons' Weddings

DEBORAH ROSENBERG

OVER A hundred years ago, a loving couple, Gittel and Shmuel, lived in the small village of Grodno. They always loved the early spring when the days got longer, and they could celebrate Passover.

This year, only a few days after they had enjoyed the seder with their entire family, Shmuel's beloved father passed from this world. Gittel and Shmuel waited for the holiday to end before they sat *shiva* for him, and then they welcomed the family, friends, and neighbors into their home.

It had been cold and dreary all week, but on the last day of the shiva, the sun came out. Though still grieving the loss of Shmuel's gentle father, the couple looked forward to life returning to almost normal.

When the family, friends, and neighbors had all finally gone, Gittel and Shmuel started to put their home back in order. They put all the extra chairs back where they belonged. They returned all the books to their shelves. They sent most of the cookies and cakes home with neighbors, and they put away the last of the bottles of wine. They opened the windows wide to let in the soft spring breezes. As they were working, they heard a clunk from upstairs.

"What was that?" Shmuel asked with fear.

"Don't worry, Shmulie. I will investigate!" Gittel said.

She went upstairs.

"I don't see anything wrong," she said.

"Are you sure?" Shmuel fussed. "Did you check the closets?"

"I checked the closets. I looked under the beds. Everything is fine," Gittel assured him. She came back downstairs and patted her husband's hand. "Don't worry. All is well. Let's finish the shiva." She walked to the big mirror in the front room and reached to pull off the stiff black fabric that was still covering it.

Shmuel helped her, and when it was down, they glanced in the mirror and gasped. In the mirror's reflection, they could see their front room was full of monstrous creatures. They were terrifying creatures of all sizes—tall, small, thin, and broad. They had claws and beaks! The large ones had huge purple wings. The little ones had small wings, mottled with splashes of purple and white. They stood in a terrifying silence.

The creatures were dressed in tattered finery. They seemed to be wearing just pieces of clothing rather than entire outfits, parts of suits and pieces of dresses with lots and lots of broken jewelry. Their clothes seemed to be made of threadbare dark wools and shattered grimy silk, festooned with rusty sequins and shredded black lace. They were sad, frightening, and terribly grand.

"All is well? Gittel! I don't think so. Are those ... demons?" Shmuel shuddered.

"Those are indeed demons," Gittel agreed.

Just then, rocks came flying at Gittel and Shmuel, passed right through them, and landed in a growing heap on the carpet behind them. The couple were too shocked to scream.

Gittel cried, "Wait! Don't you remember? When we were little, my *bubbe*—Papa's mama—told us a story about demons! I thought she made it up, but she said in the weeks between Passover and Shavuot, we Jews cannot get married, so that's when demons have their weddings. Demons like to have their weddings inside our houses where it is warm and dry. When the demons first arrive, they will throw rocks at you. Do not cry out when they throw the rocks—that angers demons, and they will kill you. When the rocks stop coming, count them carefully. You will know how long they will stay by the number of rocks they threw. You won't be able to see the demons with your eyes, but you might catch a glimpse of them in a mirror or a polished tray.

"Once you know you have demons, you have to leave your house for the number of days the rocks foretold. If you can, put out a little plate of jam. Demons love jam. If you leave quietly and leave them jam, they won't kill you and will probably leave your house standing when their weddings are done. But the most important thing is this: treat the demons with respect. Demons are very touchy about respect."

Gittel thought for a moment. She decided. She turned to her husband and said, "It's good we didn't scream, and I know what we must do."

She looked directly in the mirror and searched the reflection of the room. Many of the demons stared coldly back at her, but she persevered. Finally, Gittel met the eye of the biggest, baddest, scariest of the demons. With his battered silk top hat and frayed violet baldric, he looked like the demon in charge. Gittel took a breath, planted her feet firmly, and spoke.

She said, "Lord Demon, can you wait just a little while? We can make the house tidy so that your weddings will be perfect. Then we will leave you to celebrate as you wish."

The enormous demon nodded, just once, and blinked his glinting eyes.

Gittel and Shmuel got to work. Gittel washed the shiva teacups, and Shmuel polished the good wine glasses. They swept the floors in each room, being careful not to get dust where they thought their guests might be. Gittel stepped out back and cut a small bouquet of fresh spring flowers, and Shmuel spooned a generous heap of blackberry jam into their prettiest crystal bowl. Together, they laid their favorite Shabbat tablecloth over the table and put the jam and the flowers exactly in the center.

Gittel and Shmuel quickly packed the things they would need for forty days, for that was the number of rocks they had counted.

Gittel made sure they had plenty of warm socks, and Shmuel packed his favorite books. At the last moment, Shmuel picked up a small portrait of his late father and tucked it under the socks. Then, with trepidation, but hand in hand, they left their home to the demons and went to stay with their oldest son, still in the village but a few streets away.

For weeks, music blared from the house, and lights shone at all hours of the day and night. Neighbors complained, but there was nothing to be done. Violins screeched, accordions howled, and cymbals crashed like falling pots and pans. Horrible smells of burned rat and sulfur wafted from the house, and occasionally rocks tumbled out of the upstairs windows. Neighbors speculated endlessly on what was happening inside, but there was no way to know. The celebration went on and on. No one on the narrow lane got much sleep during the demons' wedding feasts. People were cranky, annoyed, and afraid.

After weeks of this, precisely at midnight on the fortieth day, all the noise stopped. The music stopped wailing, the smells stopped polluting, and the house fell dark and quiet.

The next morning, after a lively discussion with their oldest son, Gittel and Shmuel decided it might be safe to return home. They worried what they might find there. They had heard their neighbors' complaints and the wild speculations of the village. For forty days, they heard horror stories of demons leaving a house in ruins, with crumbling walls, with furniture burned black, with long claw marks on the floors and walls.

However, when the couple got back to their lane, their house seemed all right. The windows were closed, and the curtains inside hung smooth and straight. No sound could be heard. When Gittel opened the front door, it no longer squeaked. As Gittel and Shmuel crept through their house, they were amazed. The furniture in the front room gleamed with fresh polish. The flowers Gittel had picked over a month before were still fresh and bright. The jam was gone, but the crystal bowl, intact, was still in the middle of the table on the crisp white cloth. The kitchen tap no longer leaked, and the broken pane in the back door had been replaced. It was miraculous.

Shmuel said, "Gittele! Bubbe was right! I am so glad you remembered the story, and we knew about the jam! And you were right. Thank goodness you thought to make the house as nice as we could, with flowers and our best tablecloth."

Gittel nodded as she took Shmuel's hand. She smiled at her husband and admired the cozy room. "I am glad our home is safe. I am glad the demons got to celebrate their weddings, and most of all, I am so glad that we remembered the most important thing that Bubbe said and we chose to treat the demons with respect."

ABOUT THE STORY

There are many versions of this story. I based mine on one in *Lilith's Cave: Jewish Tales of the Supernatural* by Howard Schwartz. Schwartz cites the source as: "From Edoth (Hebrew) vol.2, (1947), pp. 283-284, collected by Menachem Azuz from Yitzhak Azuz of Gallipoli." He also cites several other variants. Before reading it, I did not know we had a tradition of spooky stories, and I was inspired to adapt it with Gail Pasternack to tell as a tandem story during our maggid training. This version is included in this collection with permission from Howard Schwartz.

Rachel and the Enchanted Spring

GAIL PASTERNACK

Long ago, there was a young shepherdess named Rachel who loved spending time outdoors. Every day, after she returned the sheep to their pens, she walked home through a grove of mulberry trees. In spring, the trees would bloom with the most fragrant dark fruit, and Rachel would often stop there. She loved the beauty of the dappled light filtering through the canopy and the music of leaves rustling in the wind punctuated with birds chirping.

One day, in spring, Rachel headed home after an especially tiring day. It was shearing time, and for days she had labored to remove the winter fleece from her sheep. As she wandered through the grove, her limbs ached, and her hands were sore.

She was so busy thinking about her pain that she wasn't paying attention to where she was walking until she realized she didn't know where she was. She tried to find the path back to the road she knew so well, but instead found herself at a spring that she'd never seen before.

Clear and pure water bubbled over the rocks and glistened in the sunlight. She was thirsty, and the water looked so inviting. She cupped her hands and drank. Oooh, the water was sweeter than honey, so she dipped her hands back into the cool spring and drank more.

The water did more than quench her thirst—it filled her with vitality. Rachel flexed her fingers. All the soreness in her hands had vanished. In fact, all her aches and pains had gone. But that wasn't the only difference.

Her awareness increased. The scent of the mulberries was stronger. The sound of the wind rustling through the leaves was louder. The light shimmering through the canopy was brighter. And she no longer felt lost. She knew exactly where she was in the forest.

Rachel shut her eyes, and when she did, she heard a strange voice.

"Did you see those shadowy figures at the riverbank?" asked the musical and twittery voice.

Rachel opened her eyes but saw no one.

"You mean the demons?" chirped another voice from above her. "Oh, yes. They sent a chill through my feathers."

Rachel looked up and saw two robins sitting on a branch.

"I heard one demon talking to the other," one of the robins said. "It plans to visit that miserly man who lives on the hill tonight."

"You mean the one who buried gold under the oak tree in front of his house?" the other robin asked. "The one who never gives to the poor?"

"Yes, him. The demon plans to kill him. If only he knew that if he keeps the demon out of his house from sunset to sunrise, it will lose its power and never be able to return."

Rachel had heard of the man who lived on the hill. He was well-known throughout the village for never giving to the poor or helping those in need. She ran to the man's house, a two-story home at the top of the village's largest hill. It was just an hour before sundown. Rachel peered through the window and saw a family of four sitting around the dining table, just finishing dinner. The man put down his fork, and his wife rose to collect the empty plates.

"Hmm," Rachel said to herself. "I wonder if this man is as miserly as they say." She knocked on the door.

The gray-haired man approached the door but kept it shut. He peered through the window and scowled at Rachel. "What do you want?" he asked in a gruff voice.

"Help me, sir. I am so hungry. Please, may I have something to eat?"

"Go away!"

A young man with dark, curly hair approached the door. "Surely we could give her something."

The older man shook his head. "I have earned what we have. Let her do the same."

A young woman in a flowing, dark dress joined the father and son. "Papa, please. The girl sounds desperate. We can give her some bread."

The man turned to his two children, and his face softened. "I suppose we could." He opened the door.

Rachel stepped inside and shut the door behind her. "I am no beggar. I came to warn you. A demon will visit you tonight. If you want to save yourself and your family, you must let me help you."

"You can't expect me to believe this!"

"Are you the man who, instead of giving to charity, buried your gold under the oak tree in your yard? If you are, then you are in danger."

The man's eyes opened wide. "I've never told anyone about the gold. Not even my wife. How could you possibly know that?"

"I know many things," Rachel said.

The man led Rachel to his sitting room, and they settled into chairs in front of the fireplace. As the fire crackled, he and Rachel hatched a plan to save the man and his family. They decided to send the man's son, daughter, and wife to stay overnight at his brother-in-law's home in the village center.

Just as his family left in their carriage, the sun dipped below the horizon. Rachel shut the man's front door and locked it. Moments later, there was a knock on the door.

"Let me in, dear one," said a sweet voice that sounded just like the voice of the man's wife. "I left my wool shawl, and it is so cold. Please let me in."

The man went to unlock the door, but Rachel stayed his hand. "Look outside," she said. "Your wife is not there."

The man looked through the window, and Rachel was right. His wife was not there. No one was there. Only the shadows of night graced his front porch.

Hours passed. Again—there was a knock on the door. "Father, let me in," said a voice so like the man's son. "I'm frightened. Wolves have spooked our carriage horses and have chased me here."

The man ran to the door, but Rachel stopped him before he could open it. "Your son is not there," she said.

Again, the man looked through the window and saw nothing but shadows.

Rachel sat in the sitting room by the fire all night while the man paced and wrung his hands. Yet, all was quiet, except for the ticking of the clock on the wall. Then, one hour before dawn, there was another knock on the door.

"Papa, Papa, let me in." This time the voice sounded like the man's daughter. "It's dark, and I am so scared."

The man wept. "I must let her in."

Rachel shook her head. "She is not there."

Again, the man looked through the window, and again, there was no one there.

The man returned to the sitting room and sank into a chair. He put his head in his hands and waited as the clock ticked away for another hour.

Rachel rose from her seat and gazed out the window to watch the first rays of sunlight peek over the horizon. "The demon is gone!"

The man rushed to the door and opened it. No one stood outside his house. All the shadows were gone, and bright, morning light filled the home.

Rachel stood next to the man. "You are saved, and all because you let me, a stranger, into your home."

Soon the man's family returned home, and the man ran out to hug them tight.

It is said that after that night, the miserly man was miserly no longer. From then on, he always welcomed the stranger and helped others in need.

And Rachel understood the language of birds for the rest of her life. In fact, it was a bird who warned her when wolves were about to harm her sheep. But that is for another story.

ABOUT THE STORY

In Jewish folklore, birds often possess wisdom. There are many tales of King Solomon speaking with birds and getting their advice, yet in the original version of this story, King David gains the ability to understand bird language when he drinks from an enchanted spring. The story originated in France and was adapted for *A Coat for the Moon and Other Jewish Tales* by Howard Schwartz and Barbara Rush. It is one of my favorite stories because it shows the complicated balance between the importance of welcoming the stranger and the need to protect ourselves from those hoping to harm us. In my version of this story, a young shepherdess named Rachel drinks from the well and saves a man and his family from a demon. Adapted with permission from Howard Schwartz and Barbara Rush.

A Charm in the Red Dress

DEBORAH ROSENBERG

ABOUT A hundred years ago, Shayna lived with her sister in the prosperous town of Berdicheva. She was just past young and very beautiful. She worked as a schoolteacher, and she sang in the choir in *shul*. She and her sister had friends, family, and a peaceful home.

One year, as the holiday of Rosh Hashanah approached, Shayna realized she wanted to celebrate her five years of teaching Torah to the smallest boys and girls in the town. She decided to have a new dress made to wear to Rosh Hashanah services.

Berdicheva was indeed prosperous, but it had more tailors than dressmakers in those days. Shayna particularly admired the work of the tailor who had made all her father's suits and her brother's bar mitzvah suit. His name was Mordecai, and she trusted him.

In the first meeting to discuss the dress, Shayna was well pleased with Mordecai's skill in measuring and his excellent suggestions for how the dress might fit and drape. Together they chose a glorious lightweight wool crepe that would cut nicely into five gores and would sway and flow when Shayna chose to dance. "The burgundy, please," Shayna decided. Mordecai promised the dress within a week, well in time for Rosh Hashanah.

Just a week later, Shayna received a note that her dress was ready for the final fitting to set the perfect length of hem. Shayna brought her sister too, so Shayna could show off the new dress.

Both women admired the dress from every angle as Shayna twirled in the mirror. Mordecai, too, was delighted with the way the dress looked on Shayna. He smiled. "A beautiful dress for a beautiful woman." Mordecai again promised speedy delivery, and the sisters left the shop, laughing together.

Moments after the sisters left, Mordecai's shop bell rang again. He turned from his table, guessing that Shayna wanted to remind Mordecai of the buttons they had chosen. To his surprise, a stranger stood before him. "How might I help you?" Mordecai asked.

The stranger looked exotic. He wore an embroidered cap with gold and silver threads in patterns Mordecai had never before seen.

"I have a favor to ask," the stranger said. "You will benefit richly!"

"What is it you want?" asked Mordecai, and he wondered why his heart beat faster.

"I noticed, in passing, the beautiful woman who was just in here, trying on a dark red dress, the vibrant woman with dark hair and warm brown eyes."

"So?" Mordecai said. "What's that to you?"

"A woman that lovely should be honored," the stranger said. "Recognized."

Mordecai was becoming alarmed and turned to step into the back room.

The stranger coughed. "It's such a small thing, and I will make it well worth your time."

Despite himself, Mordecai asked again, "What is it that you want?"

The stranger reached into an inside pocket and held up a small gold coin that seemed to be embossed with the same patterns as the man's embroidered cap.

"I'd like you to sew this coin into that red dress. As a gift to the wearer, as an honor to celebrate her beauty. It's such a small favor. I will pay you well for this trifling thing."

"If it is so trifling, why will you pay me well?" asked Mordecai, who was usually no fool.

"Ah! You are a respected tailor, a busy man. It will take extra time for you to sew this coin into the dress so that it doesn't chafe the wearer or weigh the dress down and ruin its line."

Mordecai saw the truth in that. He was an excellent tailor and had clientele all over town. And it was true, the coin had to be sewn expertly and invisibly. "What are you offering me as recompense?" he finally asked.

The stranger named a sum that would take care of all of Mordecai's concerns about money for some time to come. A small coin—what was the harm if this lunatic wanted to honor Shayna, a kind and beautiful woman? She deserved some recognition. Did she not?

Mordecai said, "Yes. I will do this for you."

Three days later, Shayna came to pick up her Rosh Hashanah dress. It was perfect; the color, the fabric, the movement, even the buttons were right! Shayna paid Mordecai, kissed his cheek in thanks, and floated home with her prize.

Three days after that, Shayna and her sister bathed and washed their hair and got ready to go to the synagogue for Rosh Hashanah services. Shayna's sister, as usual, was ready first, and she waited patiently for Shayna to finally put on the new dress so they could go. When Shayna came down, she looked pale, and her hands seemed to be shaking.

"Are you well? What's wrong?" her sister asked.

"I feel peculiar," Shayna replied. "Why don't you go along, and I will follow when I feel a little better. I don't want us both to be late!"

As soon as her sister closed the door, Shayna grabbed her best shawl and ran out the back door of their home. She thought, *Peculiar hardly describes it! I feel compelled to lie to my sister, avoid services, and run to an address that I did not know I knew.*

She ran through the early autumn twilight and arrived, panting, at an austere townhouse on the other side of town. She banged on the great door with impatience and trepidation.

A man opened the door. Shayna had never seen him before, but he was dressed elegantly in a smoking jacket, silk trousers, Persian slippers, and a fitted cap covered in gold and silver threads in a complex embroidered pattern. The man opened his arms, and Shayna fell into them.

They kissed, they writhed, they moaned. Shayna could not believe she was part of this, but she could not stop.

The man led Shayna upstairs to a sumptuous bedroom lit by dozens of candles. The man tore off his clothes and reached for Shayna. To her horror, but compelled, Shayna grabbed the hem of the glorious dress to tug it over her head. She wrenched off the dress and was about to pull off her slip when suddenly, she stopped. She looked around at the room, the man, the tumble of clothes on the floor. She realized she stood in her slip in the home of a naked stranger. Aghast, she pulled her dress off the floor and scrambled into it again. The feeling, the urgency, the need, returned.

Shayna tried to collect herself. She felt the rising passion and looked down at her dress. Slowly, she took the dress off again. The stranger watched her, bemused, but did not touch her.

"It's the dress," she whispered. "The dress is making me ..."

The stranger laughed. "And you will, my dear."

Shayna looked at the dress in her hands and at the stranger. "No, I won't. I will never do as you say." She plucked up her fallen shawl, wrapped it closely around her, and fled down the stairs, still carrying the dangerous dress.

Shayna ran all the way home, chilled in her slip and shawl. She was glad that most people were still at the synagogue. She got home safely, threw the dress into her closet, and took a long, hot bath. When Shayna's sister got back, Shayna apologized for missing the service and explained that she had continued to feel unwell. Shayna's sister made tea, cut two slices of rich honey cake, and regaled Shayna with stories from the service. The sisters went to bed early, both tired from the evening.

The next morning, Shayna woke up, resolute. She had a sip of tea and one more bite of honey cake, this time with butter. She bundled the formerly wonderful dress into a parcel and walked to the office of the magistrates. There she explained, with embarrassment, what had happened.

"I think this dress is enchanted or cursed somehow," she said.

"Where did you get the dress?" the kindest magistrate asked.

Shayna reluctantly named Mordecai.

"We must talk to Mordecai!" the sternest magistrate declared.

Mordecai's shop wasn't open yet, but he came to the door when the least patient magistrate rapped on the glass. After Mordecai nervously ushered them all inside, all five magistrates started throwing out questions, creating confusion and fear. Finally, Shayna held up her hand, as she did in class when the children got too silly. Everyone stopped talking at once. Teachers have a gift.

"Mordecai," Shayna said gently, "Did someone ask you to do something to this dress?"

"Yes, but, but …" stammered Mordecai. He shut his eyes tightly for a moment and paused for breath. "He said it was to honor you, revere you. Did something happen?"

"Almost," Shayna said without looking at the magistrates. She could feel heat rise in her cheeks.

The most tactful magistrate took Mordecai aside and quickly explained what had almost happened.

"Oh, my goodness! I had no idea! I am bereft. Are you alright?" Mordecai was pale and shaking. "He offered so much money for a trifle. We have such expenses! The roof needs mending! My mother needs medicine! The children need shoes!"

Shayna took Mordecai's hand in hers. "Money comes and goes. Is the money worth your honor and reputation? I could have lost my honor, my reputation, and my self-respect. I could have broken my sister's heart from shame. I could even have lost the teaching position I love. Mordecai, I trusted you."

Mordecai started to sob, and the whole story spilled out. Even the stern magistrate was moved.

The chief magistrate decided swiftly. "Shayna, you and Mordecai will find a way for Mordecai to make amends. When trust has been broken, it takes an act of service to repair that trust. There are families in this town who are in need; therefore, you shall start making them coats for the coming winter. What say you?"

Shayna squeezed Mordecai's hand, and he tried to smile back at her. "Thank you, sir, I will do as you say. And I thank you for your grace."

The chief magistrate continued, "We will find and destroy this evil stranger in the fancy cap. He will never mislead or mistreat a woman again. Kindness and respect will triumph from the evil that put the charm in the dress."

"I will make this right," Mordecai promised.

And Shayna shouted, "Yes!"

The magistrates did find and utterly destroy the evildoer. He did not mislead or mistreat any woman, anywhere, ever again.

ABOUT THE STORY

I found this story in *Lilith's Cave: Jewish Tales of the Supernatural*, by Howard Schwartz. There are several versions, including the earliest one found in *Maaseh Nissim* from the sixteenth century in which the dress is a coat and the charm is a root. I adapted my version on the suggestion of Maggidah Gail Pasternack to give the protagonist her own agency.

The Day the Shtetl Wept

CYRISE BEATTY SCHACHTER

RIVKA CLOSED her window against the cold wind. The clouds drifted, revealing the slender crescent of the new *Cheshvan* moon. It was clear that autumn was deepening. Rivka set down the barley and potatoes she had planned for the evening's soup. She knelt to stoke the fire in the stove and thought, *Is it the month of Cheshvan already? Funny that Leybeshke hasn't come to remind me of mama's* yahrzeit (anniversary of death). *Well, maybe this year I will go visit mama's grave myself. Ah, but Leybeshke's prayers have such a way with the ancestors.*

Her sister, Bruna, burst through the door. She laughed as children swirled around her. "Mama!" they exclaimed as they peeled off coats and mittens and ran to Rivka for hugs.

Bruna kissed Rivka on the cheek. "Has Leybeshke been to see you?"

"That's funny," replied Rivka, "I just noticed the new moon and wondered why she hasn't visited yet. Mama's yahrzeit must be a few days away, and usually Leybeshke visits us two weeks in advance."

Everyone in their village of Kremenets knew that the cemetery keeper, Leybeshke, never forgot the yahrzeit of every soul resting in the cemetery. She visited you when your deceased ancestor's yahrzeit drew near and offered to visit the grave of your relative to pray for their soul. If you agreed, you would give a handkerchief, and she would promise to ask the departed to bless you and your family.

Leybeshke rapped in just the right way on the gravestone with her polished staff of golden oak, and she had a secret way to speak the names of the dead so they always responded. It was said she sang a wordless melody that arose from another world, and her abundant tears soaked the earth and comforted the souls of the departed.

When Leybeshke returned your handkerchief, still wet with her tears, you would give her a few coins. This kept her—and her orphan niece, Chana, and their two cats—fed and comfortable in their small cottage on the south side of the cemetery. And it kept the small village of Kremenets in good favor with the ancestors.

But the moon was new and Leybeshke, strangely, had not come to visit Bruna or Rivka.

Rivka said, "We must visit her tomorrow," and Bruna nodded.

The next morning was cold and bright as Rivka and Bruna walked down the quiet road, each carrying a basket for Leybeshke. Rivka's basket held a jar of dried lemon balm. Bruna's held a jar of honey from the hives she kept.

They hadn't gone far down the road when they saw Yankel the baker approaching.

"*Shalom Aleichem!*" ("Peace be upon you!") called Yankel. "Where are you two headed?"

Bruna answered, "We are going to visit Leybeshke. We expected her to visit, but she hasn't. I can't recall Leybeshke ever missing a yahrzeit."

"I am on the same errand. My *zayde's* yahrzeit is tomorrow, and she hasn't knocked upon my door. Something must be wrong!"

Together, they hurried to Leybeshke's cottage on the edge of the cemetery. Many of their neighbors milled about Leybeshke's yard, and Rivka called out, "Shalom Aleichem! What is going on? Is Leybeshke all right?"

"Oy, sad news," moaned Shlomo, the wheel maker. "Leybeshke has laid in bed three days, silent as a stone, not eating."

Rivka and Bruna rushed into the cottage. Rivka crushed dried lemon balm to make a hot, herbal tea, and as steam rose from the cup, Bruna spooned in the sweet honey.

In the bedroom, Chana, sat by the bed, trying to coax Leybeshke to sip broth. Leybeshke's lips remained closed.

Rivka placed the cup of tea on the bedside table, and she and Bruna sat next to Chana. Leybeshke rested under her quilt. Her green eyes were open but clouded and distant. Bruna took Leybeshke's hand in hers and asked, "Leybeshke, *vos iz es*? What is troubling you?"

Leybeshke gazed out the window and spoke softly.

"Bruna, Rivka, my good women, I smell the lemon balm you brought. I would know that scent anywhere. It grows wild in a meadow near your home. When it blooms, the bees come and sing in the blossoms. Every summer, I walk to the meadow and listen to them. They teach me the ancient songs of the prophetess Devorah, keeper of the bees. Every year I go there to learn the songs for calling the ancestors."

"From the bees?" asked Rivka.

"The melodies are so beautiful that I weep, and somehow my tears make the bees sing even louder. From the bees, I gather the songs of memory, for they are like keys that unlock the gates of the merciful mothers, *sharei imahot*, and with these songs, my voice can reach all the palaces of heaven, and with the palace gates open wide, the ancestors' blessings can find us way down here in Kremenets."

Rivka, Bruna, and Chana looked at each other. Was the old woman having a fever dream?

Leybeshke continued, "But this year, out gathering rue under the full moon of the month of *Sivan*, I fell and twisted my knee. It swelled badly and was very painful. Summer came, and I couldn't walk down the steep path to the meadow with the lemon balm and the bees, so I do not have the songs. My knee has only gotten worse since then, and every night, I dream of dark-gray skies that threaten but do not rain. If the ancestors don't receive our tears soon, if I cannot offer them the songs, I'm afraid for our beloved Kremenets."

"But, Tante," Chana said, "you went to the cemetery last week?"

"Last week, I hobbled to the cemetery to pray at the grave of Reb Shlomo's mother, Malkah. I rapped on the stone with my staff, I began the blessing as I always do, and when I got to the singing of her name, I knew the words, but I had no melody. And when I began to pray, I could not cry. I tried over and over, but I couldn't unlock the gates. This has never happened to me before."

Leybeshke looked at the two sisters. "I'm sorry. It's autumn, and the time for gathering songs has passed. I cannot serve the village. I have no songs. I have no tears. Perhaps it's time for me to pass my staff to the next generation."

"No, Tante!" protested Chana. "I'm not ready!"

"Hush, Chanaleh," Rivka said. "Leybeshke will return to the cemetery."

Chana replied, "But what can we do to help her find the songs?"

Rivka looked knowingly at Bruna, and they returned to the small kitchen, still bright with the scent of lemon.

Bruna spoke, "Do you remember the incantation mama taught us for blessing the hives and how she danced while she sang the prayer to Devorah? Remember how the bees would come?"

Rivka answered, "I remember."

Together they left the cottage, bringing the honey and dried lemon balm with them. They crossed Leybeshke's yard and entered the thick forest. Bruna sprinkled crushed lemon balm on the earth as they walked. Rivka drizzled a trail of honey behind her. They reached a clearing where there stood a great old stump. Rivka spooned a thin amber strand of honey over the stump. Bits of lemon balm drifted down and stuck in the honey.

Rivka took a deep breath, closed her eyes, and danced, slowly, as she remembered her mother doing. She called out, "*Ima* Devorah, wise mother whose name means 'bee'! Oh, knower of the songs, reveal the cure for Leybeshke and call your faithful servants, the good bees of this land, to sing at her window."

Silence fell in the wake of Rivka's invocation, and then, one bee appeared, softly buzzing. As it sipped some honey on the stump, another bee appeared, then another, until a small cluster of bees hovered above the stump, dipping to sip honey, then lifting again into the air.

Rivka heard the crunching of dry leaves. She opened her eyes to see her neighbors standing before her.

"Whatever magic you women are weaving is working! Can we call more bees?" asked Shlomo excitedly.

"Yes, but we have to offer our tears," said Rivka.

"You mean cry? But we never cry. That's always been Leybeshke's job," Shlomo responded.

Rivka stood up straight. "When was the last time you yourself cried for your own beloved mother or father or sang your uncle's favorite song at his graveside?"

Everyone shuffled uncomfortably.

"I always just pay Leybeshke to visit mama's grave," said Bracha the baker. "She's so good at it."

"Bracha," Bruna said gently, "I remember your mother. She was such a kind woman."

"Yes," Bracha said. "My mama never scolded us. She was so patient with us, so tender." A tear splashed onto her cheek. "She made the sweetest *rugelach*, and her hair always smelled like cinnamon." Bracha sank to the ground and sobbed.

Bruna knelt and put her arms around Bracha. They rocked softly as they both wept. The bees drifted toward Leybeshke's cottage.

"Reb Shlomo," Rivka said. "I remember when you were eight years old and broke your leg in the woods. People searched for you, and it was your beloved uncle Meyer who found you. He carried you back home, where Fruma the healer set your bones."

"Uncle Meyer sang me such a sweet, calming song as he carried me. I still remember it." As Reb Shlomo began to hum the tune softly, tears poured from his eyes. His wife began to hum along until she was crying too. Soon many were humming and crying with them.

The villagers all told stories, recalling their mothers, fathers, grandparents and even beloved children who had been lost. The bees hummed louder, and more and more of them drifted toward Leybeshke's window.

Then the people heard Leybeshke's unmistakable voice coming from the open window at a distance, where a hundred bees hovered. The buzzing softened as Leybeshke's voice grew stronger, and the people moved closer to her window. With her eyes closed as if in a trance, she sang a wordless melody that seemed to wander up to the heavens and then come cascading down to earth over and over.

The group gathered close, weeping as they listened to Leybeshke's song.

Suddenly, Leybeshke opened her eyes wide. "Chana, we must go to the cemetery. I have the songs now!"

"But your knee, Tante?"

"Reb Shlomo will pull me in his wagon. Please fetch my staff for me."

The weeping villagers carried Leybeshke to the wagon. The bees swarmed ahead in a buzzing cloud, leading the strange procession up the road to the cemetery.

At the cemetery, Reb Shlomo lifted Leybeshke and set her gently on a bench beneath a gnarled oak tree. The bees rose into the branches.

Leybeshke spoke, "You must each find your beloved's resting place and speak from your heart. Let your tears water the earth, and let your beloved hear your weeping. Ask the Holy One to bless their soul and ask your ancestor for whatever healing you need."

The softest rain fell as villagers wandered through the gravestones searching for their ancestors. Their mingled weeping became a symphony of sorrows.

When they returned to the old oak tree, with puffy eyes and open hearts, Leybeshke stood.

She took her staff and tapped a slow, steady rhythm. "*Ribbono Shel Olam*, Master of the Universe, *Ima, Chay Ha Olameem*, Great Mother, Life of all Worlds! As it is written in the Psalms, '*Min Hameitzar Karati Yah!*' Out of the Narrow Places, I call to you! In the merit of our ancestral mothers, Soyre, Rivka, Rachel, and Leah, please hear the prayers of your children who have come here to weep and remember today. They weep for their mothers, their fathers, their sisters and brothers, even their own beloved children. Oh, Great Source of Blessing, allow the breaking open of their hearts to cleanse and heal us."

She continued tapping her steady rhythm as she closed her eyes and, at last, sang the melody the bees had revealed. As the last note hung in the air, the rain stopped, and the sky pinked with the setting sun.

When she opened her eyes, the villagers were standing before her. One by one, they spoke.

"Leybeshke, your cheeks are so rosy!"

"Your eyes are bright with such a brilliant light!"

"The Holy One has heard your prayer. Your voice is clear as the nightingale!"

"You're standing so easily, Leybeshke. Your knee is healed?!"

Leybeshke smiled. She stretched her arms up high. The bees rose from the branches and departed single file. Stretched like a ribbon in the sky, they made their way back to the hives behind Rivka's farm.

Leybeshke clapped her hands together. "As it is written in *Tehillim* (Psalms,) 'She who sows in tears will reap in joy.'"

Then she looked at Chana. "I hope you will warm up your delicious chicken soup when we get home. I am hungry!" With that, she started a joyful song, took Chana's hand, and walked easily down the hill with the sniffling villagers trailing behind.

From that day on, even though Leybeshke's prayers were potent and constantly in commission, the villagers of Kremenets also remembered their ancestors with their own tears. And in that way, the departed souls of Kremenets were satisfied and blessings rained, like sweet honey, upon the village for many years.

ABOUT THE STORY

This story was inspired by the research of Kohenet Annabel Cohen, who has translated *yizker bukhs* (memorial books) of the shtetls of Eastern Europe from Yiddish into English, highlighting in particular the spiritual roles of women in these communities.

In the yizker bukh of Kremenets, the *zogerke* (female prayer leader) and cemetery keeper, Leybeshke, is recalled. Cohen's translation of the book describes how Leybeshke would assist the grieving. Leybeshke would lead them to the grave of the deceased, rap on the headstone with her staff, call the name of the dead, and facilitate the connection with the person who had come to pray.

Cohen's translations inspired me into daydreams of Leybeshke as I worked in my garden one summer. That is where this story emerged.

Angel in the Candle Flame

CASSANDRA SAGAN

MY NANA, Lillian Westman Mandel, danced in her pajamas and strummed slightly off-key ukulele tunes, made up stories, and starred in living room musicals. She was a muse, a holy clown, who taught me how to live simply, and to simply love. Nana showed me how to find the portal through which to pass between this mundane world and the world beyond, pulsing with mystical tickles.

If she were here while the *Shabbos* candles cast dancing shadows, her tale would unfold into the night. Nana would be so old, her hair would have turned to snow. She'd rock gently, as if praying, her face transforming like an empty sky, slowly, and then suddenly, filling with birds. She'd begin to whisper-sing her story:

When I was a *shaineh maideleh*, a pretty little girl, and a modest one, I was blessed to spend a whole week with a Shabbos angel who slipped through the portal where Shabbos angels descend to bless us with a kiss on the *keppe*, right on top of our heads. If you gaze at the candle flame long enough and squeeze your eyes, you can see that tiny doorway. But that blessing, like everything else, had more than one side.

It was Friday night, and my family sat in the glow of the candles singing *"Shalom Aleichem"*—Come to us, angels of peace, bless us with peace—but just as we were about to sing the last verse, a ruckus erupted outside of our window.

Two skinny racoons had cracked the gate of the chicken coop, and Goldie and Gila and Lola and Laila were screeching, squawking, and flapping, banging their beaks on the metal roof.

We grabbed buckets and bats, frying pans and broom handles, running toward the coop, screaming, howling, clanging until the racoons gave up and slunk away.

And the chickens, *oy*, the chickens! We had to comfort and examine each one. *Baruch Hashem,* thank God no one was hurt, except Shmegegge, who had a tiny cut on one wing.

Our Shabbos best were now filthy, so we washed up and finished dinner in our pajamas. What a treat! The food was delicious cold, and we devoured *kreplach* and brisket and noodle *kugel.* Oy could my mother—your great-grandmother—cook. Before long, the candle flames began to sputter, and I closed my eyes and waited for the kiss on my *keppe*, which my *bubbe*, your great-great-grandmother, always told me occurs the moment the candle flames flutter out and fade away.

But that night was different than every other Shabbos, before or since. I felt the tickle-kiss of the angel, but when the flame disappeared, instead of leaving, the angel hopped onto my shoulder and settled down. The only one who noticed was Bubbe. She raised her eyebrows and nodded.

The angel stayed with me the whole week! It felt like I was in a daytime dream, a girl in a fairytale riding on moonbeams, bathing in starlight. Such a blessing, it was the most amazing week of my life.

But like I said, there are two sides to every blessing. Because to tell you the truth, the angel was a total *nudnik*. Twenty-four hours a day, she perched on my shoulder asking strange questions: "When does water sleep?" And, "What is the sound of salt?" And, "How many grapes can you fit into a rainbow?" And, "If clouds could talk, what would they say?"

But whenever I tried to ask the angel a simple question, all I got was excuses. I asked, "What is your name?"

The angel said, "We do not have names—we have spirals." And, "Our names are sounds undetectable to human ears." And, "We feel our names in what you might call your solar plexus. Or maybe that is your toe? I don't really know anatomy." And, "Our names are constantly changing."

That angel had nothing but excuses.

When we went out to feed the chickens and check on Shmegegge's wing, the angel would fire off questions to the chickens as if there was no difference between a bird and a human.

"Do tears have yolks?" And, "What is the difference between a star and a wishbone?" And, "Which color is the most ticklish?" Goldie, Lola, Gila, and Laila cocked their heads quizzically, but Shmegegge only shrugged her injured wing and sighed.

Then it was Shabbos again. The moment we lit our candles and began to gather the light, the angel hopped onto the wick, and when the candles burned down, the angel sailed on a slender thread of smoke to kiss me one last time on the keppe, then vanished into the air.

"Bubbe," I gasped. "My angel is gone! Why did my angel leave me?"

She cuddled me close and said, "*Totskele*, little one, let me tell you a story.

"Shabbos angels are like newborn babies. Every Shabbos is their first, their only Shabbos. Unless we give them the instructions to come, to bless us, to depart, they don't know what to do."

Bubbe went on: "They don't have a *siddur*. We are their prayer books. When we sing 'Shalom Aleichem,' we invite the angels to come and bless us with peace, and in the last verse, we tell them to go away in peace.

"Last Shabbos, when the racoons attacked the chicken coop, we forgot to sing the last part of 'Shalom Aleichem' instructing the angels to depart in peace. There was no way for the angel to know what to do! The angels dance all the way from heaven to our Shabbos table, to bless us with a little kiss on the keppe. That's a lot for a newborn." Then Bubbe kissed the top of my head.

With Nana's story now told, I imagine her kissing the top of my head and the tops of my grandchildren's heads. And then, like on every Shabbos, I'd reach up and kiss the top of her head, her hair so white, it had turned to snow.

ABOUT THE STORY

Shalom Aleichem is traditionally sung around the Shabbat table, and many people wonder why we dismiss the angels a few verses after inviting them to join us. To me, this prayer extends from the beginning of Shabbat until *Havdalah,* the end of Shabbat. I searched in vain for stories about the Blue Angel which I love watching dance in the candle flames. Finding none, my Nana muse and I created this one.

An Honored Guest

DEBORAH ROSENBERG

MY BROTHER was coming to visit, and I had no bed in my guest room. The bed that had been there went with Cousin Toby when she moved out. The room had been nearly empty for a year, just plants and a sewing machine, and it finally felt like time to renew the space.

After exhaustive internet research of beds, bed frames, and bed kits, I wanted something simple and uncomplicated. I decided to enlist the help of my highly-skilled sweetie, and together we built a beautiful bed frame out of cedar and fir. We attached a headboard that I had bought, given away, and bought back. I ordered the same kind of comfortable mattress I had on my own bed, bought new bedding, and we assembled a cozy, peaceful guest room with a custom-made, elegant, and comfortable bed. It was beautiful!

One night, I could not sleep and began thinking of my great fortune in this life. I live in a safe and comfortable home; I have food in the refrigerator, tools in the garage, plenty of warm clothes, great friends, a loving family, and a supportive community. I remembered a great-great-grandmother I once met in a vision. I saw her standing in a small barren room, made of damp, gray stone. She stood before the cold hearth of her home. She was dressed in filthy layers that failed to keep her warm, and her boots were cracked and worn. She looked out with a face of hopeless despair and held a big iron pot that contained only five shriveled beets. It's all she had to feed five children and a bitter husband. There was nothing else.

I thought about my lovely new guest room and wondered if my great-great could know what awaited her children's children in America: food, shelter, clothing, opportunity, and hope. I decided I would bring her here, to my house for a night of rest in my new guest room. Unconstrained by space and time, I could share what I have.

So, I invited her—or perhaps summoned her—to my new guest room. It was night already, and I turned on the small desk light to warm the room. She appeared quite suddenly and seemed surprised to be there. She looked slowly around the room, and her eyebrows shot up. I wonder how it looked through her eyes. My great-great was so weary, bone weary, that she let me take the iron pot and put it down. I helped her unwind the shawls and unpin her skirts. I unlaced the terrible boots and laid them all aside. I pulled back the bedcovers and helped her inside. She turned her head on the soft pillow, took a big breath, and fell instantly asleep. I pulled the covers more snugly around her shoulders and lightly kissed her hair.

While she slept, I made some changes. Since we had stepped out of time, linear or logical, I worked peacefully. I washed all her clothes: the simple shirt, the rough-woven skirts, the shredded petticoats, the endless shawls. I patched the torn places with fabric that magically matched. I replaced her threadbare socks with thick new ones. I conjured new boots of oiled leather that would better fit her feet and protect her from the cold. When all of that was done, I looked at the big iron pot.

Five shriveled beets would not go far to feed a family of seven. I knew she had no pantry or larder with more, so I decided to supply abundance. I filled the pot with all the vegetables I could think of that might grow where she lived—carrots, potatoes, onions, cabbage. I slipped in salt and pepper. I told the pot that these had to be renewable items, so that every time the pot was emptied, it would refill. I asked the pot to adjust to the seasons—more potatoes when it was cold, more carrots after the summer harvests. I asked the pot to maintain its own fire and to bank the coals at night to keep the house warmer. The pot gladly agreed to all my requests. It had suffered too.

When my great-great grandmother woke up, I brought her a steaming cup of cocoa and a slab of bread and cheese. She looked rested and refreshed. Her eyes were bright, and there was pink in her cheeks. She devoured the food. After she ate, I showed her the shower and handed her a new bar of soap. She laughed as she stepped under the warm spray. I heard her singing a song I thought I recognized. "*Schluff mine maidele ...*" (Sleep, my little one.)

When she was done, I handed her my fluffiest towels. She stroked the fabric in wonder. Finally, we dressed her in her clean clothes and new boots. She smoothed her skirts and smiled widely. She had dimples!

When she was ready, we prepared to say goodbye. I don't know what she thought of the whole adventure. Perhaps she assumed it was a dream. She said nothing, and I chose not to speak either. We looked at each other for a long time, and I realized that our eyes were the same shape and color. She laughed and touched my cheek, and I hugged her tightly. We each closed our eyes, and I imagined her back in her home, with the big iron pot beside her, brimming with hope.

When I opened my eyes, she was gone. The bed was neatly made, and the room was exactly as it had been before.

Sometimes, late, when I cannot sleep, I check from time to time to see how she and her family are doing. With better food, the family's situation has improved considerably. The children talk and play. My great-great-grandfather remembers how to smile. Everyone is stronger with energy and stamina. The older children helped their parents build two more beds so that all the children have places to sleep, and my great-great grandmother can at last share a bed with her husband. They have repaired the gaps in the walls and the missing panes in the windows. The littlest girl, my great-grandmother, brings home flowers from the fields and adds color to the house. The children go to school and bring home stories to share. Now, before Shabbat, my great-great-grandparents and all five of the children clean and cook and prepare so they can sit down together at the new trestle table to share delicious soups and stews. They sing. They laugh. As a family, they talk and wonder and make plans for the future. The iron cooking pot refills every day with seasonal adjustments, as requested. There is enough to share with neighbors who have since become friends. A collection of houses has become a community.

Do I actually believe that my great-great-grandmother spent a night in my guest bed? Is it possible that an iron cooking pot delivers fresh produce to the past? Against all reasonable thought, I know she was here, and I know that pot keeps its promise. Can we alter the past and create a better present—even a better future—for ourselves and our families? I am sure that we can. We just need to imagine what is possible and make it so.

ABOUT THE STORY

A few years ago, I had the opportunity to participate in extraordinary healing work with a counseling facilitator and a client. The facilitator and client chose a traumatic experience in the client's childhood, and then the three of us enacted the events with different, positive outcomes. The work was powerful, and the client was helped immeasurably. That work inspired this possibility.

Contributors

Debra Gordon Zaslow was ordained as a maggidah by Zalman Schachter-Shalomi, *z"l*, in 1995. She travels nationwide telling stories and leading workshops in storytelling and writing. She holds an MFA in writing from Vermont College of Fine Arts, and she taught storytelling at Southern Oregon University for thirty years. Her CD, *Return Again,* features Jewish healing stories, and her memoir, *Bringing Bubbe Home, A Memoir of Letting Go Through Love and Death,* chronicles midwifing her grandmother through the passage of death. She runs a maggid training program with her husband, Rabbi David Zaslow, in Ashland, Oregon, and together they lead Shabbat weekends across the country.

Gail Pasternack is a writer, storyteller, and educator, who was ordained as a maggidah by Maggidah Debra Gordon Zaslow and Rabbi David Zaslow in 2021. Her writing has appeared in *Jewish Fiction.net,* the *New Mitzvah Stories for the Whole Family* anthology, *Wanderlust Journal,* and *The Fruit of Yitzhak's Tree* anthology. Since 2015, Gail has served on the board of directors of Willamette Writers and led the organization as its president for five years. A native New Yorker, Gail and her husband now reside in Portland, Oregon where she enjoys drinking cocktails, listening to live jazz, and dancing Argentine tango.

Deborah Rosenberg has been a professor at Southern Oregon University for over twenty years. She came to SOU from New York where she worked as faculty costume designer and costume shop supervisor at Ithaca College and SUNY Brockport, as well as guest draper at Cornell University and resident designer at Niagara University. Professional costume design credits include the Alley Theatre, Player's Theatre Columbus, the Berkshire Theatre Festival, Shakespeare and Co., and theatres internationally. At SOU, Deborah teaches costume design and stage makeup. She holds a BA in anthropology from Trent University in Ontario and an MFA in costume design from North Carolina School of the Arts.

Lisa Huberman (they/them) is a storyteller, educator, performance artist, Jewish art nerd, and plant parent based in Baltimore. Raised by vegetarians in Ohio, they spent twelve years in New York City making theatre and Jewish ritual in synagogues, black box theatres, living rooms, and rented church basements. As a Jewish educator, Lisa has worked in large communities like Congregation Beth Elohim in Park Slope Brooklyn and Adas Israel Congregation in DC, as well as innovative start-ups such as Malkhut and the Wandering Jews of Astoria in Queens. Their storytelling projects have been featured at La MaMa Experimental Theatre Company, Mission to (dit) Mars, Dixon Place, Project Y, and have been funded by the Queens Council of the Arts. Lisa has also published personal essays about Jewish identity and pop culture in *Hey Alma* and *Tor.com*. They received maggid ordination in 2021.

José de Kwaadsteniet finished her studies in theology in 1986, being a student of Rabbi Yehuda Aschkenasy, z"l. After a few years teaching rabbinics at a Dutch university and co-editing a book about the Shema, *With Unbounded Love Have You Loved Us*, it turned out her health had other plans with her future. Then, in 2000, she became able to do some studying and teaching again, which she both loves and has done since. After coming out as a Jew in 2014, she teaches Torah and midrash to people who are also in the process of converting to Judaism. She is a member of the progressive Jewish congregation Beit Ha'Chidush in Weesp/Amsterdam, The Netherlands.

Cyrise Beatty Schachter was ordained as a maggidah by Maggidah Debra Gordon Zaslow and Rabbi David Zaslow in 2021 and as a teacher of Jewish meditation in 2004. She has led Jewish communities as musical director, Shaliach Tzibur, and rabbinic assistant for the past twenty-five years. She holds an MFA in writing from San Francisco State University and has been published in several anthologies. She is the founder of Living Language, a summer immersion program in creative writing for girls. Cyrise teaches classes in music, Judaism/feminist theology, and hip-hop dance from her home base in Ashland, Oregon, and across the country.

Cassandra Sagan has devoted her life to helping others access their creative brilliance. A twice-ordained maggid in the lineage of Reb Zalman Schachter-Shalomi, and ultimately the Baal Shem Tov, she is a consummate cultural creative: educator, poet, singer/songwriter, visual artist, an InterPlay leader, creator of Moving Midrash, an embodied Torah study practice, and a regular "Joy Gevalt." She has been published in a wide variety of anthologies and journals, and taught in classrooms, synagogues, libraries, and retreat centers for most of her life. Cassandra weaves her tales with humor and magical realism, while making ancestral *tikkunim* (repairs) through her characters and story lines.

Batya Podos received maggid ordination from Rabbi David Zaslow and Maggidah Devorah Zaslow in 2012. She directs Congregation Nahalat Shalom's education program in Albuquerque, where she brings stories to life in the classroom and the Jewish community. She was co-mother of Abraham's Tent, an interfaith summer camp for Jewish, Christian, and Muslim children. She served on the faculty of the Jewish Spiritual Education program and co-directed the RISE Storytelling Initiative. She is the director of the NM Jewish

Storytelling Festival. Her first novel, *Rebecca and the Talisman of Time*, was nominated for the Oregon Spirit Book Award. Her second novel, *B'one Deep*, came out on Amazon in 2024.

Ayala Sarah Zonnenschein was ordained as a maggidah in 2014 by Maggidah Debra Gordon Zaslow and Rabbi David Zaslow. Since then, she has been part of the leadership team at Congregation Havurah Shir Hadash in Ashland, Oregon, leading/co-leading Shabbat and holiday services and telling Jewish stories. She has been the executive director of Havurah Shir Hadash since 2013.

Melissa Carpenter, at the turn of the millennium, fell in love— with the Torah. She started writing and delivering Torah monologues at P'nai Or of Portland, Oregon; took biblical Hebrew at her alma mater; and began sharing her own commentary in her weekly blog, Questioning Torah. In 2009, she completed ALEPH's two-year Davennen Leadership Training Institute to improve her lay leadership, and in 2012 she was ordained as a maggidah by Debra Gordon Zaslow and Rabbi David Zaslow. Today Melissa is still writing her blog, teaching a class on the Torah, and telling Torah stories.

Rivkah Coburn has been weaving Jewish storytelling into her teaching and leadership as long as she can remember. As a dancer, choreographer, and Jewish embodiment facilitator, Rivkah's storytelling style infuses a magical physical quality with the sacred, delighting the inner child of any age. Thirteen years after receiving ordination as a maggidah from Rabbi David Zaslow and Maggidah Debra Gordon Zaslow, with blessings from Rabbi Zalman Schachter-Shalomi and the Holy One's help, Rivkah received her rabbinic *smicha* in January 2025, through the same lineage of the ALEPH Ordination Program.

Acknowledgments

This was a group project, and I am immensely grateful to all the *maggidot* (Jewish women storytellers) who enthusiastically collaborated on this book from its beginning, and those who joined later by contributing stories. Special thanks go to Gail Pasternack and Deborah Rosenberg, who worked tirelessly with me on the details for two years. Without Gail's editing and technical skill, this book would not have happened.

I want to thank all the authors and storytellers who gave us permission to use stories from their collections as blueprints for our adaptations: Howard Schwartz, Peninnah Schram, Barbara Rush, Steven Zeitlin, David Holtz, and Carole Forman for the Estate of Yitzhak Buxbaum, *z"l*. I am grateful to Cherie Karo Schwartz for her sage advice and consultation on all aspects of story.

Thank you to Cassandra Sagan for the use of her art for our book cover. Many thanks to Ali Shaw of Indigo Editing, Design and More for editing in the early stages, and Jon Sweeney of Monkfish Publishing for guidance and editing in the final stages. We are grateful to the whole team at Monkfish for putting the book together. Lastly, I thank my husband, Rabbi David Zaslow, for his unwavering support throughout this process, and throughout life.

www.ingramcontent.com/pod-product-compliance
Lightning Source LLC
Jackson TN
JSHW022314270725
87828JS00001B/1